A WINTER'S ROSE

TANYA ANNE CROSBY

OLIVER HEBER BOOKS
A QUALITY BOOK PUBLISHER

COPYRIGHT © 2018 Tanya Anne Crosby

Published by Oliver-Heber Books

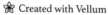 Created with Vellum

PRAISE FOR TANYA ANNE CROSBY

"Crosby's characters keep readers engaged..."

— PUBLISHERS WEEKLY

"Tanya Anne Crosby sets out to show us a good time and accomplishes that with humor, a fast-paced story and just the right amount of romance."

— THE OAKLAND PRESS

"Romance filled with charm, passion and intrigue..."

— AFFAIRE DE COEUR

"Ms. Crosby mixes just the right amount of humor... Fantastic, tantalizing!"

— RENDEZVOUS

"Tanya Anne Crosby pens a tale that touches your soul and lives forever in your heart."

— SHERRILYN KENYON #1 NYT BESTSELLING AUTHOR

#metoo

SERIES BIBLIOGRAPHY
A BRAND-NEW SERIES

ELEMENTAL MAGIK

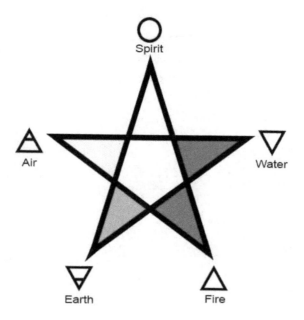

"Destiny is what I make it."
—*Morwen Pendragon*

Returning from assignment in the wee hours of the morn, Wilhelm of Warkworth reined in his mount, motioning for his companions to do the same.

The southern woods were dense with mist, and, at first glance it would appear a heavy fog had crept up from the shore, thick as usual on a balmy morning, but the taste on his lips was not salt, but ash, and the odor that flared his nostrils recalled him to the stench of greasy pork blistering on a spit.

A sense of premonition shook him as he and his men leapt down from their mounts and ventured silently forward, emerging from the woodlands to a landscape painted black.

Summer was gone; so was every trace of green that heralded that season. But the eerie silence and coal-black fields were not natural. Neither was the absence of leaf-litter, broom and mulch. In the distance, smoke curled upward from twisted piles of embers, filling the air with a stench that permeated everything it touched.

Gone.

Everything was gone.

The devastation was staggering. Every alder, ash and elm within range of the castle had burnt to nubs, some still nurturing flames. The castle on the motte had been a temporary measure, constructed mostly of pinewood and spruce, making use of the area's most prominent woods. Sparing only the outbuildings surrounding it, the edifice was consumed.

Only six months ago, they'd begun construction on a new stone wall to replace the wood palisade; now that was all that remained. And, if there was life to be found within a hundred yards of the motte, it wasn't immediately evident. It was only after the trio ascended the hillock and Wilhelm picked his way through simmering ruins that he spied movement inside the bailey. Survivors lifted ash-covered faces as he approached, pausing from their searches to reveal eyes that were red-rimmed from tears and smoke. But it was the cook he happened upon first. Bearing a carcass atop his bent shoulders, he came marching out of the ruins.

"What happened here?"

"They came like thieves in the night," said the old man.

"Who?"

"The Count of Mortain with his Welsh witch."

Morwen Pendragon.

Terror shook Wilhelm to his bones. "My fa—Lord de Vere? Where is he?"

The elder man lifted a bony shoulder, peering back into the destruction in a gesture that sank Wilhelm's soul. He turned again, and the old man's dirty lips quivered as he hoisted down his burden, laying the ravaged young woman down amidst a growing pile of dead. He straightened the woman's twisted body, then smoothed her half-charred dress. "I found her in the motte," he said.

His heart wrenching painfully, Wilhelm looked closer. *Oh, nay, nay, nay...*

Lady Ayleth.

He recognized her only by the silver cross she wore—a cross he, himself, had given her as a consolation when Giles de Vere left for the seminary—not that Wilhelm would ever dare covet the lady for himself. He simply hadn't liked to see her pining so long over Giles. He'd hoped the cross would give her comfort. Now, the horror of her condition brought a lump of bile to the back of his throat. Her once lovely face was covered with ash, half peeling away. At the grisly sight, some unnamed emotion overtook him, and he felt like ripping the cross from her neck. But he did not. Hardening his heart and ordering his companions to help, he abandoned his horse where it stood and marched into the ruins himself, reassured that no one would dare relieve Lady Ayleth of her valuables. At six-feet-five and weighing more than sixteen stone, Wilhelm Fitz Richard, bastard son of Richard de Vere, and Hammer of Warkworth, was no man to be trifled with—particularly not today, when everything he'd held so dear had been wrenched from his life.

The scent of death rose with the morning sun, the odor of decay growing thick with the humidity, until the stench was caked into every fiber of his being.

Alas, as the day wore on, he continued to drag out bodies, putting them aside to be given a proper burial. Skin charred and sliding off bones, it gave him a heave to the belly every time he hauled out another, but he was duty bound to persevere—at least until he found his lord sire and brother. And then, though sadness might have easily consumed his resolve, he felt the burden of responsibility. At forty, he had been the youngest of his father's sons, save for Giles, and in one fell swoop, he'd become the eldest, with two half-sisters gone, and an older brother as well.

Roger de Vere had been the pride of his father's heart. Now, the firstborn son of Warkworth lay desecrated beside their lord father, and it fell to Wilhelm to look after Giles—St. Giles, they'd called him, not because he was a saint, but because, as a boy, Giles de Vere was more in love with his books than he was with his steel. Unlike Roger, Giles had never aspired to lead Warkworth's armies, nor did he concern himself with carrying on his sire's name. But he was the only one who could. Neither Wilhelm nor his progeny could inherit these lands, nor did he bear the lord's name. His mother had been a lowly servant—well-loved after the death of de Vere's first wife. His second wife —bless her soul—lived but long enough to give birth to Giles. And the third... here she lay.

Wilhelm dropped his mistress's fragile arms, wondering how her Scots-loving sire would fare with news of her death. Their youngest daughter—younger than de Vere's youngest child—was good and dead. Arms akimbo, he glared down at the lady's body, scarcely recognizable in its wasted state, but suddenly, he spied the gleam of silver clinging to her charred finger and he bent to retrieve the sigil—a lion sejant holding in his dexter-paw an axe, and in the sinister, a tilting-spear. It was a perfect match to his father's, a smaller, more delicate version of the lord's ring. Both now belonged to Giles—the weedy brother he hadn't seen in years and who'd broken Lady Ayleth's heart.

Examining the ring—a sigil that would never belong to Lady Ayleth—he stood considering the brother who'd never loved her and felt a prickle of envy... and... a needling sensation at the back of his neck, almost as though someone could be watching... and then laughter. *Hideous laughter.* Distant and spine-chilling, the sound clearly mocked him.

You will never inherit, because you are unworthy... from dust you were born, to dust you will return... forgotten.

Closing his fist about the silver and gold bejeweled sigil, Wilhelm's dark eyes studied the landscape—the still smoking fields, the distant glitter of the ocean...

There was nothing out there... nothing... and yet, as the ring cut into the tender flesh of his soot-stained palm, he still heard it... the tittering of fate for a man who'd dared to love where he should not...

Unworthy, the voice said. *Forgotten.*

"What is it?" asked Edmond, who'd ridden back with him from Reading and then worked tirelessly beside him all night long.

"'Tis naught," Wilhelm said, shaking it off, attributing the gloom to his grief. And still, he felt a hovering darkness that unsettled him to his bones. "I would have you ride for a priest," he said. "St. Giles must be told, but I cannot scribe the letter myself."

"Bamburgh?"

"Might as well."

"Will he come?"

The glow of the raging fire must have lit the night sky for leagues, and yet, no more than six leagues away, the lord of Bamburgh had never bothered to dispatch men to their aid—not even for the sake of his daughter.

"He'll come," said Wilhelm. "If only to shrive his daughter. 'Tis Lady Margaret who lies at my feet."

Both men peered down at the fire-wasted body, and when Edmond lifted his gaze, Wilhelm nodded, opening his fist to reveal her sigil ring. "All accounted for now," he said. "Lucy, Alice, Roger, my Lord de Vere, and..." He looked down at the barely recognizable corpse, giving it a nod. "...Lady Margaret. No one has survived."

For all the hope his father bore, Warkworth was now without a lord. Even if the Church agreed to dispense Giles, there was no guarantee King Stephen would give him the seat, not if his father had been declared an enemy to the crown.

Edmond scratched his head, averting his gaze, looking as though he might weep and perhaps, he would, because his thoughts had clearly ventured in the same vein Wilhelm's had: They were lost without a lord. Edmond returned his watery gaze to Wilhelm, and said, "Well... we still have Giles, right?"

There was little wonder it was phrased as a question. Despite that this was now Giles de Vere's birthright, he might not agree to leave his Church, not for a pile of rubble and bones.

"Go on... fetch the priest," Wilhelm said, with no small measure of disgust. "Then, while you're at it, get on your knees and pray to God Giles has what it takes to see our lord avenged."

Only after Edmond was gone did he mutter for his

ears alone, "If he does not, I will." And he glared at the motto on the lady's ring. It read: *virtute duce comite fortuna*—led by virtue, with great fortune.

It was their family dictum.

But not anymore.

1

F lanked by two of his men, William d'Aubigny, the earl of Arundel marched into the King's Stables. Not only was he Stephen's loyal man, he had doubtless had some hand in the burning of Warkworth, and realizing as much, Giles de Vere stopped short of the stable yard, eyeing his elder half-brother with no small measure of concern. He slid off his mount, intending to avoid a confrontation at all costs. So much as he loved his sable, a row with Arundel would prove infinitely more troublesome. His brother would tear the king's pet apart and their dispensation would be denied long before their bargain could be ratified.

Thankfully, Wilhelm didn't notice the man. "We can't leave the horses here," his brother complained. "We're not so poor we can't spend the coin to stable them properly."

"They'll be fine," Giles reassured, although he wasn't entirely certain that would be the case. "We'll be in and out before the sun sets." Anyway, he reasoned, the stable hands were well accustomed to handling the surplus. Already, a stableboy had spotted them and was on his way.

By the saints, his brother was as loyal as they came, but already he had a bee up his bum. If Wilhelm were to have his way, they would walk into the king's hall, wielding torches, and set the entire palace to flame—an eye for an eye. But patience and cunning were far better options. Such things were better finessed.

Vengeance is mine, I shall repay, saith the lord.

Reluctantly, Wilhelm slid off his horse. "If you say so, but do me a favor, Giles: Whatever he says in there, don't trust the pillock. Mark me, if you bring that witch home, she'll report everything we do, and once, again, Warkworth will be left in ruins."

Less than five months after the fire that had ravaged their lives, Warkworth was well in the process of being restored, but doubtless the king already knew this. It could well be that they would slap Giles in irons even before he had the chance to stand before Stephen, and, regardless, if they did not leave with the dispensation, there was every chance all the work they'd accomplished would be undone. As it stood, Warkworth remained defenseless.

Waiting for the stableboy, Giles lowered his voice, urging Wilhelm to do the same. "You must trust me," he said.

"I trust you. I do not trust *her*."

And regardless, the bargain was made. Nothing Wilhelm could say would sway him, and there was so much more at stake than just Warkworth. "I promise you, Will, I'll keep the lady in her place."

Clearly unappeased, Wilhelm's scowl deepened. "She, too, is a witch, Giles. Did your seminary teach you so little? How came you to the foolish notion that you could bend such a woman to your will?"

Both men fell silent and the look on Wilhelm's face

was fierce as Giles handed over the reins to his sable. Undaunted, the boy peered up at Wilhelm and said, "Happy Yule, m'lord. Dunna worry! I'll keep 'em safe."

Impressed, Giles smiled at the lad. There weren't many grown men brave enough to speak to his brother whilst he wore that churlish look on his face. "See you do, lad, and I'll pay another ha'penny each."

"Yeah, m'lord," said the boy excitedly, and he stood waiting while Giles pried the lead out of his brother's hands.

He waited until the lad was gone and then said, "If you cannot control yourself in the presence of *our king*, I wouldst suggest you find yourself a pub to drink away your woes whilst I go bargain for the return of our keep."

There was no question; they would avenge their kinsmen. But one thing at a time, and right now, Giles needed that dispensation to build. Without it, all his plans would be thwarted.

Wilhelm mumbled something unintelligible, though Giles understood him anyway. His elder brother and self-appointed guardian would never willingly abandon his side, but God help them both if Wilhelm should open his mouth. He prayed the bloody fool would find the strength to at least attempt to hide his loathing. Only once they were far enough from the stables, he reassured him again, "You must trust me, brother. I know what I am doing."

"And if, by chance you do not, you will die in there today, and if you do, Warkworth will be lost."

As true as that might be, it was a risk Giles was forced to take. For his own part, he would have had done with the entire affair, and walked away, leaving vengeance for its own time and place, but there were too many who depended on him now. Whether he liked it or nay, the titles and lands were his to command. And yet, make no mistake, he did not like it. He had never aspired to be lord. His eldest brother had spent the entirety of his life training for the day he would inherit Warkworth—Roger was the one who'd earned the right to wear the sigil now adorning his little finger. But without Giles, the seat would be lost, and without the seat, there would be a weakness in their defenses. His brother didn't have the bloodline to hold it, nor, in truth, did it serve Wilhelm that he'd been his father's emissary, stealing messages to King Henry's widow at Arundel.

Adulterine castle.

How those words galled.

They had far more right to their *adulterine castle* than Stephen did over the chair he occupied. Henry himself had awarded those lands to his sire. He hadn't taken the seat per force, only to live his life anticipating betrayal at every turn—and rightly so perhaps. The king's own brother—the same fool who'd awarded Stephen the keys to the trove—was now rumored to be courting the Empress Matilda behind his back.

Greedy, feckless liars, all of them.

And, even so... Giles had no stones to throw, because he, himself, was going into the king's hall with every intention of defying Stephen in the end—and God have mercy on his soul.

God have mercy on Eustace if Giles ever faced him.

The atrocities the king's son had committed—not only to Warkworth, but across the realm—were unspeakable, and it was one thing to slay one's rival in combat, yet another to lay waste to an entire *donjon* full of innocents.

The suffering his poor sisters must have endured was enough to make Giles rage against the heavens and put a fist to the ground in defiance of all he'd been taught. Their sweet faces haunted him ruthlessly, and despite that he hadn't been there to witness their end, he saw it all through his brother's eyes. Even five months later, Wilhelm's fury burned hotter than the embers he must have picked through the night of the fire. Sixty good souls were lost that day, and it was impossible to forget to grieve whilst they were still cleaning up debris.

Perhaps equally as much to bolster himself as to remind Wilhelm of their purpose, Giles halted before the palace door. He turned to face his brother, reaching out to put a calming hand on Wilhelm's shoulder.

Giles, himself, was a good stature—six-foot-one and fourteen stone—but his brother towered over him still. "Will you, *please*, try to control yourself?"

Wilhelm frowned, clearly piqued over the fact that Giles would endeavor to instruct him at all. Lord or nay, Giles was the younger son, the one less fit. He was the boy their father never even once considered as his heir, and for all intents and purposes, Wilhelm was far more suited to the position.

"Dunna worry. I'll keep my gob shut," Wilhelm promised, and Giles lifted a blond brow.

"And your dirk?"

Traces of a smile tugged at his brother's lips, but he nodded nonetheless. "Aye... the dagger stays where it is... lest there be an apple to peel."

Giles coughed to conceal his laughter, and he looked at his brother sternly. "You *must* trust me," he entreated again.

"'Tisna you I'm worried over, Giles."

And yet, it was, and if Giles weren't in such a rush to be done with the entire affair, he would have argued, because, after a fashion, Wilhelm must not trust him at all.

There had been enough words spoken between them for Giles to know that Wilhelm did not feel Giles measured up to the task ahead. And nevertheless, he recognized fear in his brother's countenance, and guessed the truth: Wilhelm wasn't so much angry; he was afraid—for Giles. Because this was the first time since the burning that they would be forced to stand and face their tormentors. Wilhelm must fear he had been summoned to his death. And, after all, who could say it wasn't so? If, indeed, Stephen had a mind to, he could take Giles' head, or imprison him, and give Warkworth to any man of his choosing. It was well within his bounds to do so, even if it might not be fair. But, the one thing they had going in their favor was, of all things, the very devastation Eustace had wrought upon their lands. There weren't many barons who would think it a boon to be offered a ruined estate, just a stone's throw from unruly Scots. And yet, to allow Warkworth to slip to the enemy would be the gravest of mistakes. Despite that it lay less than thirty miles from Bamburgh, it was not destined to be another gem in Scotland's crown. Warkworth's location was crucial to England. The bulwark would give Stephen a much-needed foothold in the north and a significant port of entry. Without Warkworth, there would be no allies to man the northern shores. But it would take gold to rebuild—gold other barons might not spare, but gold Giles had aplenty.

So, this was the carrot Giles had put before the ass: Give us the dispensation to rebuild, not of wood, but stone, and Warkworth will serve *God's anointed sov-*

ereign. So it was agreed. Although, in addition to his fealty, Giles also promised to take a wife of Stephen's choosing—and this was the bee buzzing up his brother's bum: The daughter of Morwen Pendragon, the witch who'd burned their home and murdered their kin.

Alas, there was so much he wished to say to his brother, and so much he could not. And barring that, he smiled, clapping Wilhelm on the shoulder. "Should we walk into a trap, I give you leave to take as many heads as you like."

"For Warkworth," whispered Wilhelm, another smile tugging at the corners of his mouth.

Giles nodded. "For Warkworth," he returned, and between them, the whispered words were as much a call to arms as any they might have uttered on a battlefield.

Very somberly, the brothers turned to walk into Westminster Palace, where Giles de Vere was prepared to bend his knee to the Usurper...

For Warkworth.

2

Rap. Rap. Rap.

The knock on the door was tentative, perhaps even diffident, but if there was one thing the Ewyas sisters had learned since arriving at court, it was that the king's household lived in fear of Morwen Pendragon. Such as it was, there was a note of dread in the voice that called to them from behind the door. "My ladies?"

Seren, Arwyn and Rosalynde each exchanged nervous glances, for *this* was the moment they'd been anticipating. Downstairs, Morwen was in attendance with Stephen, interrogating their sister's intended.

Would he insist upon taking Seren with him?

Regardless, it could be the last time the sisters would be all together. Of the five, Rosalynde and Arwyn were the youngest of their brood—twins born minutes apart. Seren was the middle child, and Elspeth and Rhiannon were the elder, with two good years between them. Rhiannon was still in Wales, imprisoned, or dead, so they feared. Elspeth was far, far to the north, wed to an enemy of the crown, and from what little gossip they had gleaned, she was being held against her will, forced to wed the mendacious traitor Malcom Scott. Of course, Rosalynde suspected there was more to the story and she believed Elspeth had embraced her *magik* in her darkest hour.

"Lady Seren," the woman called again. "Please, please hurry..."

As luck would have it, this would be the first time since arriving in London that Morwen's manservant had left them unattended. Certain that her daughters knew better than to defy her, Morwen had sent Mordecai out to run some errand—no doubt she had sent him to murder some unsuspecting soul.

As Seren plucked her cloak from a chair, Arwyn opened the door to reveal a pinched-face matron behind it. The woman peered into the room, searching for Seren, and then seeing her, said with a note of relief in her voice, "The king beckons, Lady Seren. You must hurry."

"I am ready," she told the woman, gesturing for Arwyn to open the door a little wider. Then, whilst the woman waited, she went to each of her sisters, kissing them in turn—Rosalynde first, as she was closest. They put their heads together, and Seren whispered. "I love you, dearest sister. Remember this always." And then, whispering lower, she said, "Get the Book as far away from here as possible. I shall delay her as long as I can."

Rosalynde swallowed the lump that rose in her throat. "Take good care," she said. "And please, please take heart: Even if he insists you go with him, we are committed to this endeavor—all of us. It *must* be done. She will be weaker without the *grimoire*."

"My lady," the woman urged from the hall. "Your betrothed awaits, and... your mother... she'll be angry."

"I am coming," said Seren patiently, realizing the

maidservant was not to be blamed. She was merely doing the king's bidding, nothing more, nothing less.

With trembling knees, Rosalynde stood watching as her sister moved to kiss Arwyn next, and as her sisters embraced for the last time, she plucked up the small tallow candle on the dresser, preparing herself for the task to come.

By the door, Seren affected an excited tone for the sake of the maid. "Worry not, my sweet sisters. I am pleased with my match, and I pray you, too, will soon find your own champions." She smiled, but her eyes shone with tears as she met Rosalynde's gaze across the room, and Rosalynde found her own eyes dampening as Seren blew her a kiss good-bye. The sisters shared one last meaningful glance, and then Rose tore her gaze away.

Arwyn's voice was tender, but raw with her grief. "Go with our love, Seren. Know that wherever you find yourself, we, too, shall be beneath the same bold stars, loving you from afar."

Without another word, Seren hurried away, and once she was gone, Rosalynde wanted naught more than to throw herself on the bed and weep, though considering what little time they had remaining before Morwen returned, there wasn't time for tears, or doubt.

Arwyn shut the door and went after their mother's spell book while Rosalynde went after the nun's garb she'd stolen two weeks past. In her pocket, there was enough of her mother's *philter* to cast one *glamour* spell, and the rest was hidden in the hem of her gown. Hurrying, she donned the nun's habit, and Arwyn laid the *grimoire* down on the bed to help her affix the wimple and veil. When they were done, she left the wimple hanging by a pin, and returned to the *grimoire* on the bed, withdrawing a small blade from the pocket of her surcoat. "Hurry," she told Rosalynde, and in the meantime, Rosalynde retrieved her candle, igniting the wick with a fire song and held it over the ancient tome.

By the light of the candle, the face of the spell book appeared strangely human, with transforming expressions. Embossed upon its surface were endless, ever-changing symbols—naught the human eye could easily perceive, but before a *dewine's* eyes, the symbols rippled and reshaped, emerging and receding into the aged black leather, like hills and dales rising and re-forming to a journeyman's gaze. Much as they'd antici-pated, the book lay pliantly before them, like a joyous bride awaiting her lover.

Over the course of these past months, Rosalynde and her sisters had visited every wondrous page and pored over the rites. The recipes were ancient, but knowable only to those who bore *dewine* blood. Unlike the *grimoire* they'd begun to make at Llanthony, this one was bound by blood *magik*, and if anyone were to open the book without right, it would appear to be no more than a ruined book of prayer, faded by age and stained with watermarks. But to a *dewine*, its pages came alive, speaking to their minds and hearts.

And now, without hesitation, Arwyn sliced the blade across the tip of a finger, squeezing a few drops of her life's blood onto the leather-bound volume.

One. Two. Three.

One by one, the glistening droplets sank into the dark vellum, as though the book itself lay thirsting for the life-giving elixir. And then, she whispered.

> A drop of my blood to open or close,
> Speak now the song of ancient prose.

Shadows be gone, words reveal
The mysteries of life my book conceals.

Like a woman in the throes of pleasure, the book
trembled. But, after a moment, a burst of smoke blew
from its pages, as though it were expiring the dust of
ages. Then, as soon as it allowed, Arwyn opened the
Book of Secrets, turning the pages until she found the
proper spell.

Ready for her part, Rosalynde lifted the candle as
Arwyn shoved the *grimoire* in her direction.

"Art certain, Rose?'

"As certain as I shall ever be."

Arwyn nodded sadly. "I will miss you."

"Not for long," Rosalynde promised. Because the
very instant she could, she would return for her dear,
sweet twin. In the meantime, she knew in her heart of
hearts that this was the best recourse. "Do everything
she says," Rosalynde directed. "Everything she says!
You *must* reassure her that you tried to prevent me
from leaving and that you knew naught of my plans."

Arwyn nodded, her violet blue eyes full of fear, because it would seem an impossible task. Of all their
siblings, the twins were closest of all. There was
hardly a thing that one knew that the other did not...
and yet...

"You *must* convince Morwen of your fury! Be her
one devoted daughter. Curse my name, if you must."

"Don't worry. I will," Arwyn promised, and
knowing that time was growing short, Rosalynde
peered down at the sacred words on the vellum—
words she had by now memorized— and held the
candle aloft, setting one hand atop the spell book as
she stared into the flame.

"Ready?" she asked.

"Ready," Arwyn said, and Rosalynde spoke the words.

> Blessed flame, shining bright,
> Aid me well in my flight.
> Unveil to all another self,
> Change the book I touch, itself.
>
> Power of three, let them see, let them
>   see, let them see.
> Power of three, let them see, let them
>   see, let them see.
> Power of three, let them...

Arwyn gasped. "Oh, my!" she said, and Rosalynde at once plucked the small mirror from the pocket of her gown, gasping as well.

Her face... it was, indeed changed.

According to the grimoire, a *glamour* spell worked best—and for longer—if it didn't have to work so hard to conceal one's true nature; therefore, she'd only used a bit of the *philter*.

Evidently, it was enough. The smooth skin of her face had given way, not so much to the leathery lines of an old hag's, but certainly to a woman's whose features had been subjected to much abuse—a broken nose, too much sun. Instead of golden-red, her hair was dark as sable. Her smattering of freckles gone, and her skin pale as parchment, though splotched, her nose too big for her face, her eyes no longer blue. They were green as a forest glade, but now they resembled her sister Rhiannon's. Alas, even on her lovely sister, those wandering eyes had the uncanny effect of compelling men to cross themselves at a glance.

So now it was time to go.

She was ready.

Tears pooled in Rosalynde's eyes, but before she could allow her emotions to run amok and turn her from her task, she laid down the mirror and scooped up the *grimoire*.

Resolved, she gave Arwyn a kiss goodbye, and said, "May the Goddess love and keep you."

Arwyn's voice broke. "And you, Rosalynde." She thrust their mother's heavy cloak into Rosalynde's arms, and Rosalynde nearly thrust it back. "Take it. You will need it. Go now, and don't look back."

Already, Seren had been gone from their apartments more than twenty minutes. Fearing for a moment that it might be the last time she ever saw her twin, she lingered, giving Arwyn one last kiss and hug.

Arwyn shook her gently. "Go!" she demanded, and Rosalynde found her strength, wrenching herself away, tossing her mother's cloak over her shoulders. With her heart hammering in fear, she opened the door to their chamber, inclining her head to the floor as she slid into the hall, holding the *grimoire* close to her breast.

3

Despite the holiday—or perhaps because of the holiday—the halls were a crush of human flesh: people awaiting audiences with the king; merchants hawking wares; clergymen stalking the halls. Even in the midst of winter, the abundant smells were disturbing—particularly for a young woman raised in the Welsh countryside. Richly adorned ladies waltzed by, drenched in Flemish perfumes, followed by men, whose clothes and bodies were perfused with far muskier scents. Though, fortunately, considering the disparity between the king's subjects, no one paid Rosalynde any mind as she rushed through the halls.

Praying her mother wouldn't read Seren's mind the instant she arrived in the king's hall, she moved swiftly through the mob, her heart thrumming like priory bells. But, thanks to the *glamour* she'd cast, her appearance was so altered that, at one point, she passed Seren in the vestibule, and even her sister, for a full instant, did not recognize her.

In fact, her mother's glamour spell was so powerful that neither she nor her sisters had ever had the smallest glimpse of her mother's true persona. For all anyone knew, Morwen Pendragon was as young and lovely as her daughters—a babe herself when she'd born them. Knowing she would outlive Henry by many, many years, she'd lied to him when she'd arrived at court, telling him she was but sixteen.

Of course, it wasn't true. So far as Rosalynde knew, Morwen was at least seventy or more.

She and Seren shared a look, and with a blink of recognition, Seren's lips turned at one corner, then she lifted her chin and turned away. Thereafter, they veered in opposite directions, Seren toward the king's hall and Rosalynde toward the palace doors.

At long last, Rosalynde slipped past the guards, emerging into the yard. Holding her Book possessively, she thrilled over the prospect of seeing Elspeth again, even if it meant leaving pieces of her heart in London. She had no doubt the journey would be long and fraught with perils, but no danger could be greater than her own mother. But Morwen was as canny as she was treacherous. If Rosalynde didn't find a mount soon and flee before Morwen chanced to discover their plot, everything would be lost.

Hopefully, Seren would leave today with her betrothed, and Arwyn would endeavor to convince Morwen she'd had no hand in Rosalynde's schemes. Luckily, her sister had a way of convincing folks everything she said was true; you might call it a *glamour* of words. No doubt Rosalynde would have preferred leaving all together, but if her sister had come along, it would have been impossible to evade Morwen. As charming as Arwyn could be, she was not very self-sufficient. Rosalynde needed to keep all her wits about her at all times in order to succeed, and Morwen would pluck out their hearts if they were caught.

Nay, it was better for her mother to believe she still had three daughters to barter away, although it wasn't likely she would ever forgive Rhiannon for her part in Elspeth's escape.

Realizing with a start that she'd forgotten to check the coins in her hem, she reached down to snatch up the heavy wool gown, not caring that she was showing all the world her ankles. She'd sewn in five gold marks, along with the *philter*, basting them in place with a bit of thread. She shook one coin free, hearing it jangle, but she wouldn't rest reassured until she touched every one, and then the *philter*. Without the herbs, she wouldn't be able to maintain her *glamour*. Counting coins, and then moving her fingers along the hemline until she felt the soft lump, she exhaled in relief and dropped her skirt. The gold marks settled with another jangle.

All is well, Rose. Don't fret.

She and Arwyn had a deeper connection for having shared so much time in the womb. For them, it was easier to *mindspeak*, but they shouldn't be taking chances—and this was precisely the reason Rosalynde couldn't take her.

Find a horse. Get out of the city.

Please, shut your gob!

It was late afternoon, near about the hour when many of the king's guests should be departing or seeking beds for the evening. For obvious reasons, Rosalynde would prefer not to have to enter the king's stables. Getting back out without getting caught might be problematic. Therefore, if possible, she planned to liberate one of the horses whose misfortune it was to be hobbled outside. There were too many visitors to expect that everyone should be able to stable their mounts as they pleased. And besides, the interior stables were expensive, and often, visitors preferred to pay a stablehand to keep an eye on their belongings.

Searching for such a horse, whose groomsman was preoccupied, she walked along the stable's perimeter.

"Good day, sister."

"Good day, my son," she said, feigning a look of perfect serenity, in hopes that it would bleed through her *glamour*.

"Excuse me, sister," said another man, as he bumped into her.

Rosalynde tried not to scowl at the man, but it wasn't easy, considering that she was blessed with more temper than any of her sister's, save Rhiannon. "Good day to you," she said, though she longed to smack him with her book for not watching where he was going.

He apologized, Rose. Don't engage every battle.

Alas, Arwyn, you stole my share of good temper in the womb. But, please, do not fret, I know what my task is. I'll not risk it by engaging in petty squabbles.

Good, said Arwyn. *Good. May the Goddess bless your travels.*

Do not worry. I'll get the grimoire to Elspeth as quickly as I am able—unless your prattling gets me in trouble with mother.

And still, her sister persisted. *Do you really think she can keep it safe?*

Only pray she can, Rosalynde replied. *If not, we are all doomed.*

Their mother must be stopped. If, in fact, she continued with her present scheme, England itself would find itself beneath her thumb, because Eustace was naught but a greedy little boy.

Be safe, my sister.

I will! Now, please! Stop talking to me!

Rosalynde tried to close her mind, but distracted as she was, when another clumsy fool bumped into her—this one without a word of pardon—the *grimoire* flew out of her hands, landing in a pile of dung.

Literally.

See what you did, Arwyn!

There was only meager comfort in the fact that Arwyn did not respond. Dismayed, Rosalynde gasped when she saw her dung-covered *grimoire*.

"Nay!" she said, kneeling in the dirt to begin wiping it off—praying with all her heart that her mother would not somehow sense her betrayal and fly out of the palace to catch her on her knees—only then, it might be a propitious position from which to beg for her life.

Goddess please!

Grimacing with disgust, she attempted to dislodge the horse-dung with a finger, grateful it wasn't fresh, but it was nevertheless disgusting. With a groan, she slid the book across the dirt... and that's when she spotted the twin black horses hobbled side by side...

Like shining gifts from the Goddess, there stood two lovely mares with glistening black coats. She needed only one. And... as luck would have it, there was no one near the horses, and the stableboy was busy arguing with another customer.

Scooping up the *grimoire*, Rosalynde bounded to her feet. Not quite daring to place the book against her breast, she nevertheless held it close and made her way toward the horses. Mild mannered, neither protested her approach, and thankfully, both still wore their tack, though it was certain that neither of the saddlebags would contain anything of value. Stifling the urge to peek inside—because that might look suspicious, she pretended as though she knew what she was doing, untethering one of the horses, and apologizing to the other as she did so. Feeling a pang of regret when she led the animal away, she reassured herself that these were the gifts the Goddess had provided, and who was she to look a gift horse in the mouth?

Quickly, she opened one of the satchels, slid her *grimoire* inside, patted the mare's soft, black rump, and hurried away. When she was out of the line of sight of the stable hand, she tried to mount. It wasn't so easy as she would have supposed...

Cursing beneath her breath—because it wouldn't serve her disguise to be running about spouting oaths —she tried twice before removing her mother's cloak. Vexed with the garment simply for existing, she shoved the monstrosity into the saddlebag, not caring if it was ruined. At any rate, it was temperate for winter, and it would be easy enough to cast a warming spell—she knew plenty of those after so many years living in such mean quarters at Llanthony.

Alas, until now, she had never stolen anything of value, but the Book of Secrets was more precious than any crown jewel, and in the wrong hands, more lethal than Stephen's Rex Militum. So long as she had the Book in her possession, she must have faith and press on. No matter what... she must do all in her power to defend the Book of Secrets.

Finally, she placed her foot in the stirrup and without daring to look back to see if anyone noticed, she settled her rump in the saddle, prepared to risk life and limb to keep the Book safe, she snapped the reins and made for the city gates.

It was a long, long journey north, and there was no time to lose...

4

Squeezing past the hoard still waiting to air grievances to the king, Giles was more than ready to be shed of the palace.

Certainly, it was possible that, in his day, Henry Beauclerc had had nearly as many plaintiffs, but Giles couldn't imagine a single body more constrained by those walls. And to make matters worse, there were so many people in attendance that the air was spicy with scents—not a one of them recalling him to frankincense or myrrh.

"It smells like a dirty twat in here," groused Wilhelm, his mood growing surlier by the instant.

And yet despite his annoyance over his brother's persistent rancor, Giles's shoulders shook with mirth. It did, indeed, smell like a dirty twat.

At last, they emerged into the yard—*fresh air, at last.* And yet, even then, Wilhelm's face twisted with disgust and his shoulders remained taut enough to bounce a penny off. "You should be relieved," Giles said. "You never relished the notion of bringing *her* home, anyway."

Nor had Giles, in truth, but that was neither here nor there. Morwen Pendragon had pressed her advantage, and when all was said and done, King Stephen gave into the lady's fervent demands, sending Giles home without her beauteous daughter, but with the promise of a title and the dispensation to rebuild—so long as he agreed to bend the knee. He was to return six months hence to kneel and take his bride.

"Relieved?" said Wilhelm, casting a glance over his shoulder at Giles. "He made you earl, Giles—*earl,* for the love of Christ! For what reason, but to appease you so you might sooner kneel, and now you certainly will."

Wilhelm bolted past him and Giles narrowed his gaze on his brother's back, restraining his temper. Finally, at long last, they would arrive at the crux of Wilhelm's rage. Giles had been back now for four months, and his relationship with his half-brother was no less contentious than it was on the day he'd arrived. Wilhelm questioned his every edict and Giles was at a loss as to how to address the matter, since he couldn't glean its cause. But, until this instant, it hadn't occurred to him that his loyalty might be in question. "So, then, you think the gift of a title is enough to make me forget his son murdered our kin?"

"Don't forget Lady Ayleth!"

Giles screwed his face. God's save him; he loathed to confess that he'd been gone so long he couldn't even remember Lady Ayleth's face. And despite this, he mourned her as he did all Warkworth's wasted lives. He only wished Wilhelm would stop baiting him, as though her name were a battle cry meant to rile him against Stephen. They were already on the same side, even if he couldn't share everything he knew. "Nothing has changed, brother. You may continue to sneer and despise our king at will, but I am compelled to look the man in the face and pretend an alliance I will never honor."

Wilhelm said nothing, and Giles continued. "In the end, I, too, will have forsaken all my oaths—and worse, because at least Stephen must have believed his lies when he spoke them to Henry."

Put precisely so, there wasn't much to argue over, and to his credit, Wilhelm remained silent, though Giles wasn't yet through. "Simply because I was not there to cart out those bodies does not mean I cannot imagine the atrocities committed. I grieve for them as much as you."

If he did not openly weep—it wasn't his way—his losses were just as profound. In the space of a single night, both their lives changed.

Wilhelm marched before him, quickening his pace, and Giles said in a moment of pique, "You may have known him longer, Willie, but *I* am Warkworth's rightful heir."

"And well do I know it!"

"By the saints!" Giles snapped. He lurched forward, reaching out to snatch his churlish brother by the sleeve of his tunic, yanking him back. "What in God's name ails you, brother? Have I not done all you've asked and more? Before this is done, I will have given up my very soul for this cause."

And this was hardly an embellishment. If he told Wilhelm what price he'd paid to be released from his obligations, Wilhelm would shed blood tears.

Wilhelm closed his eyes and thrust a trembling hand to his mouth, clearly overwhelmed, and Giles realized only belatedly that he must have been walking away so vigorously, not because he was furious, but because he was in danger of unmanning himself with tears.

"I... I am... not... angry... not with you," he said.

Giles stared at him, confused. "What, then?"

"'Tis that..." His brother swallowed visibly, his brows slanting sadly. "I feel... less... a man... for having stood in that lady's presence... I did nothing." He shook his head with despair.

Giles furrowed his brow. "Lady Seren?"

"Nay, Giles! Morwen Pendragon!" Clearly, whatever it was that had unsettled Wilhelm in the hall had shaken him to his bones. It took him a moment before he could compose himself, and then said, "It was her, Giles. *I felt her that day.* Only I did not realize. I took it for my own rage, but I felt it again today—a presence black as night."

The lady of Blackwood was, indeed, quite formidable. Her gaze had never left them in the hall. "I understand," Giles said.

"Nay, brother, you do not!" Fear turned Willhelm's pupils to pinpoints. "It was as though she were here..." He thumped a finger to his head, hard. "In my head. Laughing all the while."

Giles nodded, squeezing his brother's arm, realizing only belatedly how much this ordeal must be weighing upon him. He cast a glance toward the stables, considering the holiday. Already, the crowd had thinned. "Come," he said. "The horses can wait. Let me buy you an ale for the journey."

"Piss water!" complained Wilhelm, sliding a hand down, and squeezing the tendons at the back of his neck. "I would defy you to find one good alesman amidst the lot."

"I know a place," said Giles, reaching out, pulling his brother in the direction of Castle Tavern. Finally, Wilhelm relented.

From where they stood, it was but a short walk. Regrettably, the establishment was as much a rubbish heap as he'd remembered, but at least they served their clientele quickly, and being so close to Westminster, they had better ale than most. After a drink to settle Wilhelm's nerves, he would remove his brother from this hell pot and the journey home was bound to be more pleasant.

Twenty minutes later, they were seated at a table in the dimly lit common room, clinking tankards. "To father," said Giles.

Wilhelm gave a rueful nod. "To my... Lord de Vere," he said, "May God rest him in peace." And then he raised his glass a little higher, offering a hint of a smile. "*And,*" he said, "to the newly appointed earl of Warkworth."

Giles reached up, clinking his brother's cup, meeting his gaze and holding it fast. "I give you my word, Will... I will avenge our dead."

"Aye," his brother said, flicking his nose with a finger. "I know you will." After a moment, he swiped the back of his sleeve across his suds-covered lips, and the two of them drank awkwardly.

Their relationship had never been close, but over the past few months it had been strained in a way it had never been before. In so many ways, they were strangers—too far apart in years to have any fellowship or shared memories. And, in some ways, Giles was more a bastard son than Wilhelm, because, at least Wilhelm had had their father's praise and he'd had a mother. Giles had come into this world a babe without a breast to suckle, and he'd scarce recovered his strength by the time he was old enough to train. By the age of ten, Richard de Vere had dismissed him as an able warrior. Far more readily, he'd embraced Wilhelm, who, from the first had shown a warrior's aptitude and a willingness to learn.

Their father had been a proud man, with a penchant for siring daughters. His first wife bore him a son—Roger—but then she gave him a daughter and died with her babe. His next wife gave him two daughters before Giles, then she, too, died. And if there was one thing to be said about the elder de Vere, it was that he was persistent. He married again to the youngest daughter of the Bamburgh's lord, just before her father bent the knee to David. Ayleth was her cousin.

But as for his sons... he hadn't known what to do with Giles, who was sickly until he'd sprouted his first whiskers—and in the end, perhaps more to distract him than aught else, his father encouraged him to academia. That, more than aught else, was what drove Giles to the seminary, to excel where he thought he might—for the same reason Wilhelm and Roger worked so hard in their training: to make Richard de Vere proud. None of his sons were immune to that aspiration. Richard de Vere had been a force of nature, magnanimous and ever-ready with a smile—but hard on the field, because he'd understood the consequences of frailty and inexperience. His own father had fought in the People's Crusade, and he himself had fought by Henry's side during the Battle of Tinchebrai in Normandy.

So many years Giles had watched his brothers, wishing so much that he could match them, and absurdly, it was whilst he was attending the seminary that he'd discovered, though he did have a mind for academics, he was equally adept with his sword. Simply because he'd quit Warkworth did not mean he'd quit the desire for his father's approval. He'd trained in private, and all that time he'd spent watching his siblings and father spar had not been in vain. After a time, he'd found himself enrolled in a very elite Papal Guard—so they'd claimed, a good warrior understood the value of *both* his pen and his sword. If he was now solidly built, it was due to the vigorous training he'd received, but only once in his life had Giles ever spied the glint of pride in his father's eyes—and it was a day that would haunt him till his dying breath... not simply because he'd finally earned his father's praise, but because... on that day he'd also sealed Warkworth's fate.

God's truth, he was equally responsible for the deaths of Warkworth's innocents, and even so, given the same circumstances, he would do it all again. And if he was pleased to have been raised to earl, it was only because it would better afford him the opportunity to see justice done.

Wilhelm raised his glass with a slow, unfurling smile. "Another toast... for Roger, who's like to be howling in his grave over hearing his weedy brother made earl in his stead."

A short rumble of laughter escaped Giles, but he shook his head. "Weedy?" he said, tipping his cup, and peering over the rim. He paused before putting the tankard to his lips. "Weedy?" he asked again. And yet, there was no malice in the insult, and so he let the jibe pass, wondering if Wilhelm must be blind. They held gazes a long, awkward moment, and then Wilhelm shrugged.

"'Tis been overlong since ye been home, Giles... I'd warrant Roger's got nay memory o' ye looking as ye do."

"Dead men haven't any memory," said Giles, and

Wilhelm lifted his face to reveal the torment in his gaze.

"Even so," he said, raising his cup higher. "A toast to Warkworth's firstborn. Seems unfair... to work so bloody hard... only to die the way he did." Wilhelm shook his head, peering down at the table. "I mean you no insult, Giles. But here you are... earl..."

"To Roger," Giles interrupted, eyeing his brother pointedly. The last thing he wished was for Wilhelm to say something in his cups that he might regret... or worse, that Giles wouldn't be able to forgive. As it was, he found himself subject to emotions he'd never realized he was capable of... most notably, an insidious, underlying resentment that was being stoked to life by Wilhelm's persistent judgments.

God's truth, he wished he'd known his eldest brother. For that matter, he wished he'd known his father better. But for all that Wilhelm must be grieving for everything he'd lost, Giles was also grieving for all that would never be. He had precious few memories, even of his beloved sisters, and all that remained of his brood was seated here... across this damnable table... and that man found him wanting.

Now that Wilhelm was calmer, he tried again to reassure him... after a fashion. "Remember, brother, like good *vin*, vengeance is a toast better served aged."

Wilhelm frowned.

Giles explained. "If you believe for one instant that Morwen and Eustace do not anticipate retribution, you must think again. They will look for it, day in, day out, and then... one day... when they least expect it, we will serve give our salutes from a position of power, and they will drink. Merely because I do not speak of it, does not mean I do not have a plan."

"Truly?" Wilhelm asked.

Giles reached out, clapping Wilhelm on the arm. "Truly. Have faith."

Wilhelm offered a tentative smile. "Let's drink to that," he said, and he did, tipping the glass fully, quaffing the remainder of his ale. And then he grinned—a wide, face-splitting grin that Giles hadn't seen in far too long. Pleased to see him smiling for the first time in so long, Giles ordered another round.

"For Lucy and Alice," Wilhelm said, raising another toast, and Giles declared, "Hear, hear!"

But, then, against caution, Wilhelm ordered another round. "To Lady... Margaret," he offered this time.

Three drinks in, and his brother was now grinning perpetually, even if his words didn't suit his smile. "May her father rot in hell for not coming to our aid," he said, swigging another gullet full. "I'll put him there myself if I e'er see his face."

Giles gave him a rueful laugh. "I warrant, there's going to be a crush down there already."

"So be it," said Wilhelm, slamming down the tankard. "One more!" he shouted.

"Wilhelm nay..."

His brother waved vigorously at the waitress, who, without question, brought one final round and Giles pushed his own tankard aside as Wilhelm raised another toast. "This one... to Lady Ayleth," he said, with a catch to his voice.

Giles sat back in his chair, disgusted, but not for the sake of the toast. And nevertheless, he reached out, raising his empty glass, giving the girl her due, even despite his annoyance over Wilhelm's persistence in bringing the lady up. Only then... as he set the glass down, he realized something by the look on his brother's face...

"She loved youuu," Wilhelm said, and the last word recalled Giles to a mournful howl. And, suddenly, he understood his brother more clearly—his fury and his grief, all those veiled barbs, and the constant needling...

So, it seemed, Wilhelm loved a lady who was lost to him, long before the fire. For his part, Giles had never even considered Ayleth of Bamburgh, and all these years, it must bedevil Wilhelm to know it. Perhaps he was looking for proof that Giles had not taken her affections for granted. And nevertheless, they were never betrothed, and Giles never so much as kissed the sweet girl. For all of five minutes, there had been a bit of flirtation between them, and yet, the moment Giles realized he was destined for the seminary, he'd put all his flirtations aside. So, all these months since the fire, every time Wilhelm brought up Lady Ayleth's name, he'd done so because *he* was mourning her. There was grief in his countenance now, and it occurred to Giles belatedly that he must have harbored great affection for Ayleth of Bamburgh.

Alas, if there was any trace of resentment in his tone when he spoke her name, perhaps it was because his station had prevented him from loving where he would, and it was certain Wilhelm would never have been so bold as to speak his heart; therefore, Lady Ayleth had likely gone to her grave never knowing how Wilhelm felt.

This, then, must be their nameless discord?

It had never even occurred to Giles that Ayleth had caught his brother's eye. Understanding dawned as he shoved his tankard forward, rising from his seat, anxious to be away. As the night grew colder, the inn had become nearly as much a crush as the palace, every bloke in the city filtering in from the streets, until there was scarcely standing room.

"Let's go," he said.

It was time to leave, *now*, before they turned into a pair of maudlin fools, weeping amidst London's *finest*. He skirted around the table, put his arm about Wilhelm's middle, hoisting him up. "We have a *long* way to travel," he said. "What say you we stop by Neasham?" he added for incentive.

"Why?"

"To give alms for Lady Ayleth's soul."

Wilhelm grinned, reaching one last time for his empty tankard, but Giles pushed it away. "That would be..." He hiccoughed. "Aye," he said, surging to his feet and swinging an arm about Giles' shoulder, giving him a rush of relief. The man was a bloody bulwark and if he planted his face into the table, there would be no human being alive who could remove him.

5

"As iron is eaten away by rust,
so the envious are consumed by their own passion."
—*Antisthenes*

"My, my, wasn't he a striking fellow?" I ask. "Tall, handsome, well-mannered—naught at all like the brother."

"Aye," my daughter replies, though nothing seems to discompose her. She wears a cloak of tranquility that grates on my nerves, like shards of glass in my slipper. Where in the name of the cauldron she inherited that trait, I do not know, for even now my smile is fragile and ready to shatter.

"He'll make a fine stallion. Alas, my dear, he is not for you," I say, and still, she remains silent, a pillar of genteel strength even as I grit my teeth in fury. "I have someone else in mind," I say sweetly. "Do you remember William Martel?"

Stephen's loyal steward was a rotund man, with a head like a melon, and a face only a mother could love. As of yet, he hadn't any title to his name, but as loyal as he is to the king, I know Stephen is predisposed to rewarding him, and, after all, Martel is the one man closest to Stephen, with access even to his *garderobe* and cupboards. Already once, I have persuaded him to do my bidding—when he was steward to Henry. My daughter says naught, and I continue, "Alas, he's hardly the most attractive man, but I have a use for him."

"He's twice my age," she says, finally, providing the first note of unease I detect.

I smile victoriously. "Since when does age matter, my dear? Your father was thrice Adeliza's age when he wed her—fifty-three to her eighteen, and you are older than she."

"Well, we know how that went. She bore him no children, and since remarrying for love, she has borne William d'Aubigny five babes, and counting." There was a wistful sigh in her voice. "By the by... I hear she is expecting again... apparently, that's why Lord Arundel went rushing out the door."

My daughter is a silly little fool. The only reason Adeliza of Louvain did not bear Henry any children is because *I* cursed her womb. What good would it have done me to allow more brats to his list of successors? But her silky tone grates on my nerves. A flap of nuns passes by. I smile for their sake, nodding serenely, though I am filled with rage—in truth, not so much for my daughter's forbearing as I am for Stephen's offense to me. I know that man too well. He will undermine everything I have accomplished, only to best me. Thank the cauldrons his son has more sense, and the sooner I get him on that throne, the better off I will be.

I laugh softly. "Dearest, do you think I give a damn whether you bear Martel's brats? In fact, I would greatly prefer you did not, as I will be certain to have myself named heir to your dower, in the event you should pass before I do." My smile thins, as I cast her a sideways glance. Her enduring silence does not assuage me, and I continue, "It happens all the time you realize? Only think of your dear grandmamau, taken from us all too soon."

"Thanks to you," she says, in her sing-song voice.

Alas, all my daughters are bitches, but despite Seren's confidence and even tone, I know she is unnerved.

"That man is an ogre," she says, her mettle weakening. "And nevertheless, I maintain faith in our Mother Goddess. Whatever she sees fit to provide me, I will embrace. After all, I must remember Elspeth as my example."

Elspeth.

It is all I can do not to shriek. Her very name sends a burst of heat through my veins, and if I am not careful, it will ignite the world as I pass. If I could have my eldest here before me right now, I would introduce her to suffering unlike anything she has ever endured.

My daughter.

My betrayer.

My little Judas.

How she could best me, I do not know. None of these backwater girls have ever had the least bit of instruction and whatever *magik* they possess can never match my own. Simply having *dewine* blood is not enough to perform great feats. Much the same as an archer may not find his mark with his first shot, simply being a *dewine* is not proof against failure. Even with practice, success is not assured. She must have found some wellspring to strengthen her, and I would not put it past my mother to have imbued each of my daughters with her dying breath. The thought infuriates me—that woman doted on my brats and never once gave me a bit of praise. How it galls, even now, to hear the fruit of my loins described as beauteous! Unparalleled—as though I, myself, am not gifted with the prophet's blood!

"Seren... I would caution you, my dear. Do not tangle with me, or you will find yourself twisted in so many directions you may never recover."

Again, she answers with silence—silence!—as though she must be concentrating every effort to block me.

I turn slowly, regarding her with canny eyes.

She *is* blocking me, I realize. And suddenly, as we near my apartments, I catch the tang of fear on my tongue, even as it drifts to me on the *aether*. I smell it stronger, and stronger as we approach my quarters, and I know instinctively before we arrive: Something has gone awry.

My reaction is swift as an adder's. Reaching out, I grasp Seren by the tender flesh of her arm, and wrench open the door to my apartments, pushing her inside. "What in the name of the Goddess have you done?"

Inside the room, Arwyn faces me, her face pale, and I sense both my daughters trembling as I slam the door, realizing at once that my prickly little Rose is gone.

"Where is she?"

Arwyn shakes her head and I narrow my gaze, attempting to read the girl's thoughts. Like her sister, her mind is now closed to me like a padlock against thieves.

I bristle, shifting my attention to Seren, doubling my efforts, and Seren, I realize—the tricky little witch —has mastered the art of artifice. Some of her thoughts are open to me; others have receded to the darkest corners of her mind, like little cockroaches hiding from the light. But they cannot persevere, and I will break them. And nevertheless, a frustrated growl bursts from my throat as I shove my loveliest daughter toward her cowering sister. And then... another thought occurs to me, even before the two chance to embrace—the *grimoire*.

My eyes fly to the trousseau where I have safe-guarded the Book so long. My feet do not move as I summon my mother's box. The lock clicks. The lid flies open to reveal a void that seeps into the marrow of my bones.

My *grimoire*... it is gone.

The single word that roars from the depths of my lungs is thunderous enough to bring a shiver to the rafters. *"Where?"*

"How should I know?" says Seren all-too sweetly. "I was with you!"

"Liars!" I shout. "Filthy liars!"

Suddenly there is a knock at the door, and I slam my hand down so both my daughters are brought to their knees, their beautiful faces contorting with pain as their knee-joints crack against the hardwood floors. They should be so fortunate if all I do is break their legs. Summoning all my composure, I press a finger to my lips, bidding them to silence, hoping our visitor will leave.

Seren's anger is like a crack of thunder against the silence. "I will not—"

I don't care what she is about to say. "Gwnïo ar gau!" I cut my hand through the air, viciously, whispering the words as another knock beats upon the door. And, even as I turn, I sense the stitches piercing the insides of my daughters' lips, sewing their mouths shut with invisible but infrangible threads. By the time I place my hand on the door knob, they are duly silenced, kneeling dutifully, as though preparing to pray.

"My lady," says the matron who greets me. She peers nervously within, and I, of course, have naught to hide, so I swing the door open, smiling with certainty that my daughters appear beatific in their reverent poses. I, too, join my hands together as though in prayer, and my daughters both mimic my gesture and bow their heads as I do.

"What pious young ladies," says the maid admiringly. And her brows slant with apology as she adds. "I beg pardon for disturbing you, Lady Blackwood, but his Grace begs you join him in his chambers."

It is all I can do not to shriek with despair. "Right now? Are you quite certain?" I tilt her a forbearing glance. "You see, I have only just returned from the hall."

"Aye, Lady Blackwood. I am certain. And in his present mood, ye'd best not keep him waiting."

She hasn't any clue how close I am to cutting out her tongue for daring to advise me.

"My dear, you are too kind," I say. "You must know well enough the title is no longer mine, but I thank you just as well for your deference—and your advice. Please, my dear, can you not apprise the king that I am... indisposed?"

The woman shakes her head. "Nay, my lady. He stated quite clearly that you must come at once, and—"

"And what?"

She fidgets nervously. "If you do not, he shall provide an escort."

I exhale annoyedly and turn to my daughters, cutting them a warning glance. I wave a hand to release them, and say, "Please, my dears, find your sister at once. I expect she will be waiting here, in this room, when I return."

Both girl nod at once, and, reluctantly, I move to follow the king's messenger. Alas, there is no way to avoid this summons, so I must deal with the missing *grimoire* when I return.

"Pray she is not lost," I say to them, and I know the menace in my tone is not lost to the woman at my door. She shivers as I pull the door closed behind me, and she hurries away, leaving me to follow.

Never mind... I know the way...

6

The simple fact that Rosalynde had managed to escape London without any sign of Morwen's birds was no cause for celebration. Her mother might not care so much about her, but she would *never* stop searching for the Book.

The undyed wool gown was chaffing her skin, and she longed to rip off the itchy wimple, but, until she knew for sure that no one was pursuing her, she must keep her wits about her and her disguise in place.

Intuitively, she sensed that she had already pushed the mare as far as she could for the night, and despite that she'd covered a fair distance, she couldn't have traveled more than two or three leagues. Sadly, so much as she longed for more distance between her and her mother, she also had to consider the night's precautions. Tomorrow, once she had her bearings, she could travel longer. In the meantime, hopefully Morwen would think her stupid and reckless and more than prepared to travel the night through. Then, she might not concentrate her hideous birds so near, and, thanks to Elspeth, she hadn't enough of them to do a wide search.

Was it too much to hope that she had tested

Stephen's patience once-too-oft, and he'd locked her in a tower?

Sadly, she had no doubt that, even then, Morwen would find a way to extricate herself. The scope of her influence and power was frightening.

But she couldn't worry about that right now—right now, she must find a good place to rest for the night.

By now, she was certain her mother would have returned to her quarters, and with Mordecai gone, the first thing she would do would be to interrogate Arwyn. Considering what was at stake, Rose had no doubt Arwyn would remain strong, but when Morwen didn't get the answers she sought, she was bound to be enraged and there was naught so frightening as Morwen in a fit of rage. She feared for Arwyn, but her one consolation was that if Morwen should ever harm her twin, Rosalynde would know it, and right now, she sensed Arwyn's heart beating strong.

Nevertheless, when Arwyn proved useless, Morwen would consult her crystal, and this was where Rose must depend on the strength of her *magik*.

And for this, she must thank her sister Rhiannon. Even as a wee one, Rhi had understood that someday they would all need their *dewine* gifts, and so often she had defied Elspeth, teaching them in private.

Essentially, whilst Rose and her sisters worried about being discovered by Elspeth, Elspeth had worried about being discovered by Ersinius. And, perhaps in the end, Elspeth had been right to worry, because the instant she'd left the priory, Rhiannon openly defied Ersinius—where she was now nobody knew for certain. The *aether* remained dreadfully silent—silent as these woods.

All day long she'd been repeating the only vanishing spell she knew by rote, over and over again. But, no matter how desperately she wished it were otherwise, no spell could make anyone vanish. It only dimmed one's presence to the perception of others. Sometimes it worked. Sometimes it did not. And, regardless, her simple concealment spell was not proof against the full force of her mother's *hud du*. Rosalynde's only hope would be a proper warding spell, and she knew none in practice, only in theory. For that, she needed the book. After all, the *hud* itself was one thing —it was a gift of *magik*—and the Craft of the Wise was another. Inherently, it was a practical study of the *hud*, and the *grimoire* held every recipe and every spell her ancestors had ever performed.

Guiding her stolen mare through the forest, she searched for a suitable refuge, and, at long last, she came upon a well-concealed thicket and slipped inside, leading her mare into the covert as well.

She would need plenty of space to draw herself a proper pentacle—one aligned to her own affinities, and the reason for that might prove difficult to explain, and perhaps more difficult to comprehend. There were four main elements—five altogether— and each shared a quality with two more elements.

For example, since Rosalynde was aligned to water, water was moist like air, warm like fire, but it had naught in common with earth. Therefore, all things related to the earth element lay outside Rosalynde's affinity.

To make matters more complicated, there was a fifth element, better known to her people as the *quintessence*. Borne of the spirit, this element was perfect in nature, and therefore, difficult to manipulate. But, if one did not have an affinity bordering on the *quintessence,* one could not cast *aether* spells. And regardless, only a *dewine* with a primary to the *aether* could hope to master all five. Rhiannon was such a *dewine*. Like their grandmamau, she bore the Mark of the Mother—those crossed, amber-lit eyes that distinguished her as a regnant priestess—a point of contention that Morwen had long bemoaned. No matter how powerful their mother might be, or how finely honed her gifts, she would never truly master all five elements, as Rhi could.

And yet, Morwen did have one thing going for her that the sisters did not. She dabbled with blood *magik* —strong *hud du* that neither she nor her sisters would ever have the gumption to consider. Cast with sacrificial *magik*, it was dangerous business, and a blasphemy to the Goddess.

And nevertheless, used improperly, even white *magik* could be risky. There could be no escaping the Law of Three, which dictated that all *magik*, good or bad, once unleashed into the world must return to the summoner threefold. *Nothing* occurred without consequence. It was the law of nature. For common folk consequence was no less a veracity, but for a *dewine*, whose *magik* might alter the will of gods, the consequences were more severe.

Black or white, there was a price to be paid for *magik*, and one single conjuring, no matter how well intentioned, could change the fate of nations and end innocent lives.

Alas, *magik* was not to be avoided—not today.

Realizing there was no possible way she could draw a pentagram large enough to include the horse, nor could she compel the beast to stay within its bounds, she hobbled the mare nearby, so she could keep an eye on it, yet far enough that her hooves wouldn't disturb the diagram.

Once the mare was settled, she found a sharp stick and began, as best she could amidst so much bracken, to draw her diagram precisely as she recalled, beginning with the earth affinity for a banishing spell.

Here again, the reasons were complicated. But while she had no true affinity to earth itself, the point at where she began to draw also had a bearing on the form of her *magik*.

Over these past months, she'd learned so much from the Book of Secrets, and there were essentially two types of spells to be cast: All things were either summoned or banished, accepted or denied, created or destroyed, transformed or reformed. Each of these fell under one of two elements: *aether* or earth—else, as the common folk would say, all things were under the dominion of heaven or earth.

A protection spell was in essence a banishing spell, meant to repel. Therefore, she should begin drawing her pentacle with the earth affinity at the southernmost point, because it was also her divergent affinity, then up to the west, to *aether*, across to the east, to fire, across again, to air, and up to the vertex, water, always her true north.

On the other hand, to cast a summoning spell, she would have begun drawing in the opposite direction, beginning with *aether*, but still keeping her divergent affinity at the southernmost point.

And, regardless of how she began to draw, she must always end with water at her vertex, with the properly drawn symbol, leaving her most vulnerable ingress at her feet.

Conversely, if she were to draw her pentagram with the earth symbol at its apex, it would give her no benefit.

Or, if she made the mistake of choosing the *aether*

to place at the vertex—a very common mistake, considering the *quintessence* was, after all, the most powerful of the elements—it would still leave her defenseless.

On the other hand, for someone like Rhi, whose primary was *aether*, she would always complete her pentacle with *aether* at her vertex, and water as her divergent, though, in truth, Rhiannon had no weaknesses, and once she mastered the Craft, she would be a maven of all the elements.

Alas, only a *dewine* aligned to fire did not have *some* mastery over the *aether*, and this would be the case with Arwyn. So much as Arwyn hadn't any issue with the Craft, the Craft did not love her back. She could summon a flame easily enough, but she could do little more than that. And to make matters worse, her affinity was weak and Rosalynde often feared she had somehow leeched her sister's share of *magik* in the womb. After all, it could easily happen. On the death of her twin in the womb, Rhiannon had received *all* her twin's gifts—Welsh *magik*, powerful enough for two *dewine* babes.

Regardless, elemental *magik* was complicated, essential knowledge for a *dewine*. Though simply because one *dewine* could manipulate elements, did not mean all *dewines* shared the ability; the Craft was specific to everyone. If Rosalynde were like Arwyn, whose affinities were lacking, she might concentrate on the *hud* where it enriched her... perhaps alchemy, divination, or charming.

At last, when her diagram was finished, Rosalynde attended to other matters. As soon as she could, she would ward her pentagram with a banishing spell, but in the meantime, she needed to see to the mare. At this late hour, it wouldn't behoove her to search for a burn, so she pooled her hands together, concentrating on her primary.

Already, there were particles of water in the air, and her *dewine* senses could feel them. It was no more fantastical a feat than to lure these particles together, like a lodestone with metal. And yet, no matter how many times she performed the feat, it never ceased to amaze her.

After an instant, her palm began to glisten, then fill before her eyes, and she lifted her hands to the animal's shining black lips, all the while listening to her belly grumble. There was no time for food tonight, and it wouldn't be the first time she'd gone to bed without supping.

"I wonder what your name is," she said to the mare. "You are so beautiful." And she was. Shining black as the deepest night, she would hide very conveniently amidst the brush. And, if, by chance, some predator came near, she felt certain the mare would warn her. "Won't you?" She said, stroking the sweet girl's cheek.

Rosalynde was thirsty, as well, but so long as the mare kept drinking, she kept pulling water from the air, filling her palm, knowing that once she cozied into her pentacle, she wouldn't be able to leave it again. At last, the animal seemed quenched, freeing Rosalynde to tend to her own needs. And when she was ready, she retrieved her *grimoire* from the saddlebag and knelt before the Book in the center of her diagram. She retrieved the pin she'd hidden in the hem of her skirt, pricked the tip of her finger, squeezed a few droplets of bright red onto the vellum, and once again, it vanished. Rosalynde spoke the rites to open the book, then settled in to read, ignoring the persistent grumbling of her belly.

By now, she was famished, though not enough to go foraging and risk being discovered by her mother. There were far more important matters to consider.

Skimming the pages quickly, she settled on a fire spell, and put the book down. Closing her eyes to harness the power of the emerging moonlight, she laid both palms above the facing pages until a veil of blue illumined the words. Reading aloud, she whispered...

> Goddess of light shield me tonight.
> Ye who would harm, ye who would
>   maim,
> Proceed and face the same.

A band of firelight burst at the edges of her pentagram, burning low, then diminishing. Startled, Rosalynde nevertheless continued:

> With cloth and cord of darkest night, I
>   shroud my soul.
> Light is the weapon I would wield to
>   keep me whole.
>
> By all on high and law of three,
> This is my will, so mote it be.

All of this was so new to her. She hadn't any way to know what precisely should come of the words, so she waited, listening, until she felt it—water, air and fire, coalescing all about her, binding itself to her diagram, before settling into stillness and silence. Rosalynde inhaled deeply over the feel of it. The unbridled power of nature was exhilarating, and she sensed an impossible world out there, looming. Perhaps once she and Elspeth were reunited, they could study the

Book together. With a bit of patience and practice, they might even grow to be as capable as Morwen—albeit far, far less vile. And, regardless, Rhi would be proud of her.

With a satisfied smile, she cast a glance at the mare, then proceeded to conceal her pentacle with bracken—very, very carefully, so as not to disturb the *magik*.

Although she had so much to learn about the Craft, she had more than enough practice with concealment, particularly from Elspeth. Unfortunately, the warding spell wasn't a fail-safe. It was still possible for someone to stumble over her while traipsing in the woods, and if they should happen to discover her by accident, it wouldn't serve her if they suspected sorcery—only how humorous it might be for someone to see a hapless nun sleeping in a witch's pentacle. The thought alone made her giggle, and she was still giggling as she cozied with the book beneath her cheek. She lay upon the vellum, sobering over the realization that she had so much left to do... For one, Elspeth still hadn't any notion Rosalynde was coming. Somehow, there must be some way to reach her sister without using the *hud*, but she didn't know how. Nor did she have any inkling how far she had to travel to Aldergh. And, even if she could get there safely, she hoped Elspeth would have some notion how to keep the Book safe. After all, whatever *magik* her sister had cast to protect Aldergh, it had been strong enough to make Morwen take note and withdraw.

She rolled her eyes. Her mother would have everyone believing that Malcom Scott had kidnapped Elspeth, and that some accursed malady had swept through Eustace's camp whilst they were attempting to negotiate with Aldergh's lord—a malady that coincidentally killed only Morwen's birds. In the end, Scotia's king had intervened, arriving with more than three thousand warriors, forcing Eustace's army to withdraw. But, really, Rosalynde preferred to believe that, for love's sake, Elspeth had entreated the Goddess and, somehow, her sister had summoned a powerful warding spell—the most powerful kind of *magik* of all, *magik* borne of love from the *aether*. And she knew in her heart that Elspeth would never have attempted such a thing if she'd been forced to wed a man she didn't love. Moreover, only true love could have forced Elspeth to acknowledge her *dewine* blood.

Of all her sisters, her eldest had the least affection for *magik*—perchance because she was also the one who'd been forced to watch their grandmamau burn —a penance from their mother dearest, to castigate Elspeth for wronging them by revealing them as *dewines*.

Elspeth still remembered the day Morwen abandoned them at the priory. With that hateful look in her eyes, she'd squeezed Elspeth's hand with such fury, and said, "You are the eldest. Do not be tempted. Be certain your sisters are never tempted. Remember what happened to your grandmamau? This, too, will be your fate, and my fate, should you ever dare to defy me. They will tie you to a wooden stake... and they will burn you till your skin turns black and blisters off your bones."

Poor Elspeth. Poor, poor Elspeth. What a terrible burden that must have been, and it was little wonder it haunted her still. And yet, after all was said and done, the Goddess had sent her a guardian...

Sighing over the notion, she wished with all her might that she could have a champion as well.

How sweet would that be?

Curling herself into a protective ball, she tucked her knees to her breast, lifted the veil so she could lay her naked cheek against the soft vellum, and took comfort in the feel of the soft, worn leather against her face. By its very presence, she felt the spirits of her brethren...

Tomorrow would be a bright new day.

Everything would be clearer on the morrow... and in the meantime... *defend yourselves, sisters.*

The worst is still to come.

Trying to ignore the itchy fabric of her gown and fighting the overwhelming desire to remove the wimple and veil, she fell asleep, wondering if her horse's master had yet to discover his horse was missing. It never occurred to Rosalynde to be concerned that he might find her. It was her mother she most feared, and if she could remain hidden from Morwen, what could she possibly have to fear from an empty-headed man?

How stupid must one be to leave a stableboy guarding one's horse, and, anyway, unlike Elspeth, Rosalynde had no qualms against using *magik* to defend herself and those she loved. She would call upon the Goddess in a heartbeat, and if she had a sword, she would wield it.

> Ye who would harm, ye who would
>   maim,
> Proceed and face the same.

7

Alas my LOVE you DO me WRONG
To cast ME... OFFF... discourteeeeously;
For I... have... loved YOU... soooo LONG

Wilhelm of Warkworth sang as he stumbled, punctuating his ludicrous verses with hiccoughs and burps, his voice echoing down empty streets.

As crowded as the tavern had been, the streets were deserted. Even the least pious must be home, warming themselves by a fire, eating pie and waiting for the Magi.

That Stephen would call anyone to London at such an hour was prickling to say the least, but at least Giles knew the king's paranoia wasn't particularly discerning. Even Arundel had been in the City this morn, despite the rumors of his wife's confinement. And, after all, the lady of Arundel must be content with her match, judging by the brood she was providing d'Aubigny—even while she was still passing messages to her step-daughter, though he supposed even lovely little spies had dreams of hearth fires.

His thoughts turned to Seren Pendragon.

He had no desire to align himself with Morwen's progeny, no matter how lovely the girl might be. She was naught but a lovely spy, and unlike Matilda, there was no noble cause to champion on her behalf.

Listening to his brother sing, he suffered a touch of bitterness, because, unlike Wilhelm or Roger, he'd never been the man to dream of hearth fires, but at the moment, it didn't sound so bad—a pretty wife, a warm bed...

Perhaps Wilhelm's were naught but broken dreams, but his eldest brother had been deprived of his first Yuletide with his unborn babe, and his wife. Isabel, God rest her soul, was still asleep in their bed, her belly four months thick with their firstborn when she died. Meanwhile, Roger was discovered in the garderobe. Evidently, having risen during the night, he'd fallen asleep nursing an irritable bowel. The flames must have swept through that old palisade with a terrible fury, and the irony didn't escape Giles. His brother had trained all his life to die in battle—God willing, many years after their sire—and, instead, he'd died shitting on a pot.

It was unfair, he thought, and yet, as he had discovered throughout his time in the Guard, fairness wasn't precisely the purvey of God. Otherwise, Richard de Vere would have grown fat and happy, surrounded by grandchildren, his halls ringing with peals of laughter. He sure did give it a good try. Alas, his father would never steal another sweet into a slipper. There would be no more Magi gifts for his children or his bride.

His sisters would never again titter over imagined beaus, nor would they blush over compliments, or long for springtime, when they could peek out from their windows as their father's wards brandished shining silver swords.

For all intents and purposes, Warkworth would be restored, but nothing could bring back its spirit, and Giles wasn't sure he had it in him to give his people the *joie de vivre* his father inspirited, even in a bastard son—and that, for all it bespoke, gave Giles the greatest prick of envy, because, in truth, how many bastard sons mourned their fathers so bitterly?

Wilhelm did.

For all his brother's enduring snorts and grunts and growls, he was naught but a softy, with a gentle heart, and in that instant, he resolved to be more patient with Wilhelm.

For the first time in all his living days, he felt a kinship with his half-brother—a man who'd served his father loyally, and who'd vowed to serve Warkworth's heir, even despite his endless debates.

They passed a young boy alone on the street and Giles noted his gaunt face and rags. As best he could whilst supporting his brother's uncomfortable weight, he reached for his purse found a penny, and tossed it to the boy. After all, it was the Twelfth Night, and when should a man offer charity if not on the eve of the Magi? The lad smiled as he hurried to catch the shining copper, saying, "Bless you, good sir! Bless you!"

"Bless me!" exclaimed Wilhelm. "Bless... every... one!"

"Aye," said Giles. "Indeed." After all, they had each other, and they still had Warkworth. And, if they were lucky, someday his love-starved brother would find himself another love and Warkworth's halls might still ring with children's laughter. Pleased, after all, that he and Wilhelm had found some ac-

cord, he felt better... for a time... until they returned
to the stables and found that one of the coursers was
missing. What was more, it was the sable belonging
to Giles. And what more, all the stable hands had
clearly abandoned their duties to go home and
eat pie.

"I tole ye," said Wilhelm, brandishing a finger.
"Tole ye... but ye ne'er lis—ten." He hiccoughed.

Bloody hell. Giles hated being wrong—particularly
when it concerned Wilhelm. But it wasn't just that he
knew Wilhelm would not let him live this down. He'd
paid good money for those bloody coursers and he'd
spent hours upon hours training the sable. Still,
though he was furious, he reminded himself that it
was the Twelfth Night and he had only himself to
blame. He should have known better than to leave
good horses hobbled outside the stables, no matter
the season.

God's teeth, at least they had the one remaining,
and they were lucky it was still hobbled where he'd
left it.

As God was his witness, if he was fortunate
enough to catch the thief who'd stolen his sable on the
eve of the Magi, he was going to rip out the man's
heart, because he clearly wasn't using it anyway.

With some effort, he mounted Wilhelm's courser,
then, hoisted his brother's dead weight onto the back
of the horse.

"I tole ye," Wilhelm sang again, poking a finger
into the back of Giles's head, and then, immediately
after ascending, he tumbled forward, his chin plum-
meting into Giles's back with the force of ten stone.
And then before Giles could take offense—or curse
his father for raising up a bastard so the man had so
little fear of his betters—Wilhelm drunkenly wrapped

his arms about Giles, hugging tightly as he had when Giles was six.

God's breath, would he never outgrow his brother's ribbing? He was a grown man already—lord of Warkworth, heir to his father's seat—but his elder, half-brother clearly had no fear of him. Perhaps, Giles should have provided more cause for it—after all, he wasn't the man his brother supposed. If his fellow guardsmen ever witnessed such a thing, they would piss their pants laughing. They would marvel over his patience, and then, in truth, endeavor to call him St. Giles. But it would be the last words they uttered, and well they knew it, and only the fool at his back would ever dare.

For all Wilhelm's height and breadth, Giles could easily flatten him on his back. The fact that he would not do so was because... well, he loved the sot.

Reassuring himself that it was all for the best, he settled his ire. There was no way his brother could have maintained his saddle in the condition he was in. Even now, he was clutching Giles about the middle— like some oversized maid—grinding his whiskered jaw into his shoulder.

Cursing softly, ready to be shed of London's buggery and filth, he wasted no time returning to the King's Road, hoping the bastard who'd stolen his horse would treat the lady with the respect she deserved.

They'd ridden only about an hour before Wilhelm awoke long enough to grouse. "He musta sold her... thinking... 'Why should I take ha'penny when I can fill my purse?'" He burped, the smell foul, then dropped his chin back down, catching Giles again between the shoulders. "Ye shoulda let me choke him... off," he complained.

"Save your fury for Morwen, Will."

"Alas, brother... an' ye would not let me choke her... off... either," his brother complained.

Giles laughed, though ruefully. "Not yet," he promised. "All in due time."

"Ye're too bloody soft," Wilhelm lamented, "Ye shoulda told the pillock to... piss off."

Giles sighed but held his tongue. After a moment, his brother's snores rattled his eardrums, but at least he was no longer singing and there were no more words coming out of Wilhelm's face—jibes or otherwise.

The night was cold, but not so cold he appreciated the mantle of flesh on his back, and thanks to Wilhelm's added weight, they were traveling at such a snail's pace the mare could have slept erstwhile she walked.

His brother certainly did.

God's bones, at this rate, they'd never catch their thief, but he was going to try. And still, he sighed, because Wilhelm was not his enemy; he was only a jealous fathead. And, in the long run, he wanted exactly what his brother wanted—even regarding the Lady Seren.

He no more intended to be saddled with a mole in their midst than he enjoyed riding two-to-a-saddle with the ox at his back. If only to counter Wilhelm's snores—not because he relished the season, nor because he longed for a burning Yule log, or because he was bloody glad for the company of his brother—he adopted the ear worm his brother left him.

Alas my love you do me wrong
To cast me off discourteously;
For I have loved you, oh, so long

Delighting in your company.

Greensleeves was my delight,
Greensleeves my heart of gold,
Greensleeves was my heart of joy
And who but my Lady Greensleeves.

8

Nearly half a dozen times through the long night, Giles had considered stopping for a piss and a rest.

He didn't for a number of reasons: To begin with, there was every possibility his thief would be traveling north. The deduction was elementary: He knew of an inn near-about, where the most unsavory of characters were wont to gather. There was no way to say whether his thief could be in route to this place, but there weren't many establishments along these roads, so if he found the inn, he would, conceivably, discover his thief, and then he would give the knuckle-dragger a Yuletide gift he wouldn't soon forget.

And if he didn't find his thief, there would be other stolen horses to purchase.

He followed his gut, pressing forth, never imagining how close he was, until, right before sunrise, he made a fortuitous discovery. Wilhelm may have passed on by, but Giles had a nose for his horse; her scent tickled his nostrils.

She must have scented Giles as well, because she nickered softly, and Giles reined in abruptly, dislodging Wilhelm's head.

"Wha—"

Giles elbowed his brother in the belly. "Shhhhh!" he said.

Sensing trouble, Wilhelm sat upright, sobering.

Dismounting quietly, Giles made his way toward the sound of grazing and what he discovered in the thicket hobbled his tongue as surely as *she* had hobbled his sable.

God's bones! His thief was a woman—a nun.

She lay sleeping peacefully, her wimple askew and her veil concealing only half her face. Even so, Giles found himself tongue-tied, and would have roused the girl, except... there was something about her that disoriented him.

He'd seen her face before, if only in his dreams. But nay... this girl was like a chimera—undefinable at the edges...

Tilting his head, Giles studied the nun, and couldn't say whether she was young and lovely... or if she was old and unattractive. Her nose wavered between pert and small to hooked and crooked. But... if he looked very, very intently, her skin appeared so perfect as to seem translucent...

ACHING and sore from her crude bed, disoriented from her fitful rest, Rosalynde cracked her lids and found a strange pair of eyes peering down into her face—not Arwyn's nor Elspeth's, who each had violet-blue eyes, and not Seren, whose eyes were the silvery blue of a winter sky, nor Rhi, whose eyes were gold, like a wolf's. Nor were they precisely like Morwen's eyes—so uncannily black that one could scarce see where her pupils ended and her irises began... these were the eyes of a stranger.

Squealing, she scrambled to her feet, only belatedly remembering to retrieve her book. Her heart hammering with fear, she nevertheless bent to seize it, and noticed that the man didn't bother to stop her.

He merely stared.

"Who are you?" she demanded to know.

"Who am I?" he asked, his dark eyes crinkling slightly at the corners. "You know... I wondered the same about you." He was still posed on one knee, making no effort to rise, but his gaze shifted to the mare grazing nearby.

Rosalynde blinked. "I—"

His lips curved into a roguish grin. "Perhaps the horse got your tongue?"

Rosalynde blinked, completely at a loss for words. For this very occasion, she'd had an entire fabrication prepared, but at the instant, all thought fled her head.

Fortunately, his eyes never once alit upon her *grimoire*, so he mustn't have been sent by her mother. If so, he'd have seized the book by now and probably killed her long before she'd chanced to open her eyes. Repairing the veil with a hand, Rosalynde studied him as he watched her. And still, he cocked his head as though awaiting some response.

Behind him, a movement caught her attention, and her eyes widened fearfully as she caught sight of yet another man—a giant, with arms as big as trunks and a body like an ox.

"Don't worry about him," the man declared. "My brother is harmless."

The giant rose to his full height and snarled, and Rosalynde hugged her book tighter, not entirely certain he spoke true. His "brother" was scowling at her as though he'd like to rip her limb from limb. It was all she could do not to run.

"I—" Her gaze returned to the kneeling man, who, by now, had still made no move to rise, and, in fact, he put an elbow to his knee and leaned forward, staring rudely.

His voice was smooth as honey. "Tell me, Sister, is that—" He pointed to the mare. "Your horse?" He lifted his finely-hewn chin, and Rosalynde had a terrible sense that his question was a trap. If she answered in the affirmative, he would assign his *harmless* brother to do his worst.

"Not precisely," she said, with a lift of her chin, and realizing a nun would never affect such hubris, she lowered her gaze.

WHATEVER CHIMERA GILES thought he'd imagined was gone. It was, perhaps, no more than a trick of the light.

Weary as he was after the long night's journey, he raked a hand through his hair, shaking off his fatigue.

Scarcely dressed for the weather, this woman stood shivering, clutching her book with a look of desperation that called to his heart. Her countenance was indisputably matronly, and this was meant to be kind. She had jowls, like a hound, and her nose was crooked, as though it had been broken many times. Much to his dismay, he was relieved when she repaired the veil, but it wasn't like him to be so ill-affected by anyone's appearance, and therefore, even before she began her woeful tale, he suffered the grave misfortune of feeling sorry for her, and favorably predisposed to helping if he could. "I hired a guide in London town," she was quick to explain. "Once we were on the road, he beset me and stole my purse." She shook her head, jowls jiggling as she pressed the tome to her breast. "I was afraid... so I hid."

Who in God's name would burgle a poor nun? Frowning, Giles peered back at Wilhelm, who was scowling now as well, although perhaps he was more offended that Giles would have called him harmless.

"A guide, you say?"

Wilhelm said naught, but he lifted his brow, as though to challenge Giles. But, what, in God's name would he have Giles do? Leave the poor woman distraught? She was alone, in treacherous woods reputed to be full of brigands.

"Aye, sir," she said.

"You paid him? How much?"

The nun sighed despondently. "I had five gold marks. He took it all but left me the mare."

Wilhelm gave a low whistle and Giles shook his head.

"Good Sister. Did no one e'er advise ye ne'er to travel with so much gold, especially through these parts?"

The woman straightened to her full height—not at all formidable, though her demeanor would have him believe she thought otherwise.

"Aye, sir, and yet, where do you suppose I should have left my purse?" She looked as though she might weep, even with the impertinent tilt of her head. "I left home with all I owned, to offer my worth to God."

Giles blew out a sigh. "Well... I suppose it will have to be God's score to settle," he said. "But I'm sorry to inform you that the mare is not *yours*. She is mine."

The woman's eyes widened. "Yours?"

"Aye, she's mine. So, it seems, your *guide* burgled me as well, and if God does not settle the score, I may yet tend to him myself.... only the fool will have to stand in line."

"Well!" She exclaimed, with as much animus as Wilhelm was displaying. "That fish paste!"

Giles found himself chortling. "What is your name?"

"Rosalynde."

"Aye, well, Sister Rosalynde, you mustn't fret," he said, hoping to soothe her. "We'll not leave you stranded. Only tell me, where is it do you wish to go?"

9

His dark eyes glinted, and his smile transformed his face like to that of a delivering angel's.

For a moment, Rosalynde was too dumb to speak.

There were legends that told of a distant kinsman —the Merlin of Britain, better known to her people as the prophet Taliesin. He was purported to be the most beautiful man in all the realm. For love of him, Cerridwen's own daughter had defied her witch mother, and in turn Cerridwen doomed the entire isle of Avalon to the Endless Sea. This instant, Rosalynde could well believe a face like that could change the fates... this man might well change hers.

She could scarcely believe her good fortune. She lifted a hand to her breast in surprise. "Where do I wish to go?"

"I believe it's what I asked."

But, nay. Of course, he would wish to help her. There was naught surprising about that. She was a woman in distress—and not merely a woman, but a woman of the cloth. What man worth his salt would ever abandon a sister in her time of need?

"We haven't time for twaddle," said the brother, and Rosalynde's hopes were dashed.

She looked from one man to the other, uncertain which of the two was the one in charge. For what it was worth, despite the bigger man's perpetual frown and his aggressive posture, the other man seemed more... well... perhaps dangerous—even if the other did not perceive it.

Like Elspeth, Rosalynde could sometimes read auras and the beautiful man facing her had a thin but distinct thread of black in his life force—no red, which implied to Rosalynde that whatever it was that informed his colors, it was not tied to his emotions. In other words, he could slice a man's throat, but it was not a thing he would do in anger. Fortuitously for her, she didn't sense that throat-cutting was a pastime he was inclined to, else the black in his aura would be more prominent.

Still, it was there, and it gave her pause... and she was glad now that she had taken time to conceal her pentacle. Anyone who might stumble over the diagram who did not understand the Craft might think it to be Satan's work. It most certainly was not. Simply by nature, all *dewines* were inclined to follow good Christian tenets. Their priests and priestesses were not unlike Christian priests, who in their hearts and minds were closer to God. Her grandmamau claimed all gods were one god, born of the same Great Mother, from whose very womb had sprung the world itself.

Looking back and forth between these two brothers, Rosalynde watched as the handsome man's jaw tightened, though rather than appear frightening, he was more arresting—like the graven image of a golden idol. And mayhap this was why the other one did not take him seriously: He was too stunningly beautiful to appear threatening. Apparently, only Rosalynde sensed the quiet rage burning behind his words. "You return to Warkworth. I will escort the lady myself."

"Giles."

"Wilhelm."

"Nay," said the other man resentfully. "I'll not leave you." And Rosalynde took a defensive step backward.

Giles?

Giles of Warkworth?

Wasn't *that* the name of the lord expected to wed her sister? And yet, it could not be—if so, he had clearly and inexplicably found her sister wanting, else Seren would be with him now. So far as Rosalynde knew, her sister was supposed to have returned to Warkworth with her betrothed.

Giles's dark eyes shone like tourmalines—as impossibly dark as his hair was fair. "Accompany me, or nay, I will not leave this Sister alone." He turned to cast a pointed glance at his brother and Rosalynde could feel the underlying tension mounting between them. Whatever it was that was troubling these two men, she wanted no part of it.

"Well," she said, considering her mother, "I should be going..." As it was, she feared to tarry longer, and she hadn't *any* desire to embroil herself betwixt these two siblings. Even so much as she longed to inquire about her sister, she daren't do so. "You may have the mare," she said, waving good-bye, but neither of the brothers bothered to look at her. "I'll be going!" she said louder.

"Nay!" said Giles, turning to stab Rose with a razor-sharp glare, and yet she sensed his anger wasn't directed at her. "I. Said. I. Will. Escort. You."

"Oh. Very well," said Rosalynde, as he turned again to look at the one called Wilhelm.

"And come to think of it, not only will I escort you, my brother will as well."

So now she knew which of the two was in charge... *Giles*. Giles de Vere. The very one who was fated to marry her sister. What a strange, strange turn of fate, but she couldn't decide whether it was good... or bad.

Right now, it felt more bad than good.

The tension between the two brothers was indisputably brittle. The air crackled between the pair as palpably as it had with her warding spell—which, she realized only belatedly was completely diminished. Giles must have broken her *magik* when he'd stepped into her pentagram.

Naturally, her first thought was for Morwen... if her mother should happen to peer into her crystal at the moment, there would be naught to keep her from finding Rose. Holding the book close, she frowned.

"As you wish," said Wilhelm, peering down at his boots, looking as though he might suddenly retch... and then, he did.

Rosalynde twisted her lips into a grimace and looked away.

The lord of Warkworth's toothy smile reappeared. "You must pardon my brother," he said. "His ale has gone to his head, and his manners to the devil."

Rosalynde nodded, but the greater part of her only wished she could flee—without these two men in her company. And nevertheless, she had the sense, after watching them, that there was no true discord between them. Quite to the contrary, the one called Wilhelm seemed to care about his lord brother, and she needn't read auras to know it; the truth was there in his eyes. Rather, she sensed there was a certain lack of accord creating some rift between them... and she wondered if it had anything at all to do with her sister.

These would not be the first two men to vie over Seren. Scarcely a month after their arrival in London, her sister had already had multiple requests for her hand, and two of those men had reputedly come to fisticuffs.

"I would be... grateful for your help," she said to Giles. "Thank you," she said to Wilhelm.

At the least, she must feel a little relieved for their protection. No matter how good she might be at foraging, her sisters had always claimed she had more valor than good sense.

Frowning still, Wilhelm swept a sleeve across his lips and said, "No worries, Good Sister. 'Tis but poor timing, and 'tis hardly your fault."

Still clutching the *grimoire* to her breast, Rosalynde offered the man a smile, confused by their demeanor.

"Where to?" asked Giles.

"Neasham," said Rose, a little alarmed by how easily the lie slipped through her lips. And yet, it wasn't entirely unrehearsed. After all, Neasham was run by a small sect of Benedictine nuns, founded in part by the very woman whose habit she had stolen in London—Sister Emma.

"There you go," said Giles, sweeping a hand in his brother's direction. "How convenient. We'll deliver her, with little time lost."

Wilhelm nodded, though sullenly.

"Thank you," said Rosalynde yet again, and, affecting her most benevolent tone, she added, "Because of you, my faith in men is restored." She smiled winsomely, forgetting about her *glamour* spell and both men turned away, perhaps discomfited by her smile. Rosalynde lifted a brow at the sight of their chagrined blushes, but at least she knew they weren't escorting her for the wrong reasons.

"It seems to me that your good faith in men should keep a bit of caution," Giles said, and he turned to his brother. "Go, on... prepare the horses," And then he addressed Rosalynde again. "Gather your belongings, Sister. We'll be on our way at once. But, if you do not mind, I would ride my own horse.... and you..."

He looked toward his petulant brother, who was already gone to do his bidding, and apparently changed his mind, because he furrowed his brow. "You will ride with me."

Rosalynde covered her answering grin with a hand, and it was all she could do not to giggle. He looked so perfectly disheartened by the notion.

10

F ew things in life were mere coincidences, and if there was one thing that separated the heart of a *dewine* from the hearts of ordinary men, it was that a *dewine* understood intuitively never to ignore a gift from the *aether*.

Clearly, these two men were meant to be part of Rosalynde's destiny, and she understood they were sent for a reason. She only prayed that reason would see her safely delivered to Aldergh, and to Elspeth... not to Morwen.

Considering their demeanors, she watched them both carefully. It would be just like her mother to send a beautiful demon to do her dirty work. Thankfully, she didn't get any sense of maliciousness from either of the two.

The one called "Wilhelm" dutifully inspected his brother's mare, perhaps to be certain Rosalynde hadn't somehow despoiled the beast. But despite the feeling of rancor she sensed from him, there was nothing about his actions that gave Rosalynde any indication he conspired against his brother. Rather, he very meticulously tightened the cinches, checked the length of the stirrups, adjusted the lord's saddle and patted the twin satchels. Finally, after having discovered the lump of her cloak, he peered inside the satchel, pulled out the garment, then gave Rosalynde a bewildered glance, before shoving it back down into the pack.

She had the sense Wilhelm didn't entirely trust her, though if he believed she'd lied about her circumstances, he didn't confront her. And that was a good thing because she hadn't any viable explanations to give him. For one, she couldn't begin to explain why she wasn't wearing her mother's cloak in the middle of winter, when he and his brother were heavily weighted beneath fur coats. She simply didn't wish to wear the foul garment, and at the instant, she wasn't cold. Her warming spell was burning strong.

The same might not be true for her *glamour* spell, she realized, and if she was meant to travel with these men, she must soon reinforce her spell. After all, she hadn't missed that odd look Giles gave her when she awoke—as though he couldn't quite fathom what or who she was.

Sad to say, it was impossible to know how long she had remaining before the spell faded, because she was only a novice and most of her *philters* and spells were untried.

Until yesterday, the *grimoire* had remained locked in her mother's trousseau, and she and her sisters had barely had any time to study it alone. Naturally, it was Rosalynde, with her tinkering skills, who'd learned to pick the lock, and nevertheless, during these past six months, there had been so few opportunities, and they'd only had any at all because they'd persevered, realizing that the only chance they had to defeat Morwen was to learn the Craft.

Hopefully, by now, Elspeth, too, must realize they

needed *magik* to defeat Morwen. Men alone hadn't any chance against her—not kings, nor queens, nor sons of kings. So much as the newly appointed Count of Mortain believed he had some hold over Morwen Pendragon, he most certainly did not. He was her mother's poppet, no more, and Morwen was evil incarnate. Not even Elspeth would believe it if they told her what atrocities they had witnessed at Darkwood—depravity beyond imagining. Even now, all these months later, Rosalynde still shuddered to think of it...

In her mind's eye, she saw the blood-soaked biscuits... Morwen's familiar plucking at the crumbs... those shining black eyes so full of knowing.

Forsooth, she didn't know which she feared most —Morwen, her wicked birds, or Mordecai, with his unfailing eagerness to please the Dark Witch of Bannau Brycheiniog. Alas, she could only deal with one problem at a time... and right now, the problem was her fading *glamour*...

Twice she'd attempted to slip away, twice Giles warned her against wandering. The second warning left her cold. "Of all the woodlands to choose, Sister Rosalynde, you made your camp very close to Darkwood," he explained.

Rosalynde stiffened. "Darkwood, my lord?"

"Aye," he said. "'Tis no wonder your *guide* led you to these parts. These woods have long been a haven for brigands, cutthroats, and more of the like. Rich as they might be with quarry, even King Henry wanted no part of them."

He and Wilhelm shared a meaningful look, and Wilhelm shook his head ever so slightly.

Giles turned to wink at Rosalynde. "As tempted as I am to seek out your thief at a nearby inn, I'd rather reimburse you myself than deal with that den of miscreants. And besides," he said, with a lop-sided grin, "it seems my brother is afeared."

To that, Wilhelm cut him a mean glance, but Giles ignored him. "Five gold marks, you say?"

Rosalynde nodded, but reluctantly, because she still had all her money hidden in the hem of her gown.

"Worry not, Good Sister. I will provide you the entire sum, especially since I do not intend to part with the mare. But you must be content with a few silver marks until I can send you the rest... if you will trust me."

Inexplicably, Rosalynde did trust him. Though, sad to say, he had little cause to trust her as she'd been lying to him from the very moment he'd happened upon her. "How... kind," she said, struggling with her guilt.

He would give five gold marks to a stranger he'd only just met? He must have plenty more, and never mind, because she shouldn't take a penny.

Giles de Vere *must* be a champion, indeed, and there could be no doubt he was sent by the Goddess, but... what could possibly have happened in London to change her sister's fate? Had Giles repudiated Seren?

That seemed... utterly... impossible.

There was naught wrong with Seren. Her sister wasn't merely lovely; she was as kind and gentle. She was gracious and good in all she did, and no one could fault her for anything— certainly not the likes of Giles de Vere.

The merest possibility of him repudiating her sweet sister did more than confuse Rosalynde; it tempered her gratitude, even as some terrible, terrible part of her—some part she couldn't explain and didn't wish to acknowledge—was oddly gleeful their union wasn't ordained.

But why? Why would she feel this way?

If Giles was such a goodly man, why should she begrudge Seren that boon? Rather, she should be pleased for their union, not relieved that the bargain wasn't sealed.

Brooding over her ludicrous thoughts—that perhaps Giles was not meant for her sister after all, rather he was meant for her—Rosalynde went about her woodland bower, holding her *grimoire* close, surreptitiously hoofing at the lines of her pentacle beneath the bracken.

At intervals, both men peered in her direction, casting her odd glances, as though they questioned her very sanity. But, of course, they would; what a sight she must present, looking like a hen scratching at feed.

Alas, she couldn't take any chances. Covered by bracken, her diagram wasn't visible to any but discerning eyes, but she didn't intend to leave anything for Morwen to discover, particularly so near to Darkwood—the very name gave her a shiver. All this time, unbeknownst to her, she had been headed directly toward that place, and it was almost as though her mother had been leading her to her ruin.

Even now, was Mordecai waiting for her?

What might have happened if these men hadn't come upon her sleeping?

She took comfort in this: If, in truth, Morwen had found a way to influence Rosalynde's thoughts, Rosalynde should have felt her prying. Even more significantly, it wasn't her mother's way to wait about for anything. Morwen did not take lessons in patience from the spider in a web, no matter how sticky her thread or how deadly her poison might be.

Rather, her weaknesses were pride, impetuousness, and arrogance. And, in her vainglory, she would never guess how powerful Rhiannon was growing. None of her daughters would dare reveal it, and hopefully, that realization would come too late for her. And nevertheless, before anything could be accomplished along that vein, Rosalynde must first deliver the *grimoire* to safety... somewhere Morwen wouldn't be able to reach it. To her knowledge, that place could only be Aldergh.

Hurrying as best she could, she erased all traces of her pentacle, all the while thinking about Elspeth and Rhiannon, how different her eldest sisters were.

Elspeth had been their father's favorite—more beloved even than Matilda, and if only she'd not been born a bastard, she might have been his choice to wear England's crown—not that it would have ended any differently for her than it did for Matilda. Times were never so dire as to place a woman on the throne. And nevertheless, if anyone could inspire confidence, it was certainly Elspeth. She had their father's grace, and Matilda's fearlessness, albeit without the haughtiness that plagued their father's rightful heir.

Rhiannon, on the other hand, could be as ruthless as Morwen in so many ways, cunning and cold when she must. But she was loyal and fierce in her defense of those she loved. And, unlike Morwen, she did have the patience of a spider, weaving her web so meticulously, only waiting, waiting...

Someday, Rhi must be the one to challenge Morwen, though if her sister had a plan, she'd kept to herself, and it aggrieved Rose to no end that she had so meekly allowed their mother's guards to abuse her that last night at the priory. They'd placed Rhiannon in iron shackles, tossed her into a tumbril, and to this day, Morwen refused to speak of her second eldest, and Rhi, so skilled as she might be, mustn't be able to *mindspeak* outside proximity—why, Rose didn't know, but she assumed *mindspeaking* worked like the light of a flame. Up close, it burned brightly, but the further one moved away from the source, the dimmer it became. Long ago, many, many eons before Rosalynde was born, Rhiannon claimed that folks were more accustomed to *mindspeaking*—not merely *dewines*, but everyone.

Eventually, they learned to block the ability to save themselves the grief of hearing the truth, because the heart did not always agree with what the tongue proclaimed.

Similarly, right now, her heart was telling her one thing, and her mind was telling her another.

Run! said her mind.

Stay, said her heart.

AT LONG LAST, the brothers were ready to ride, and Rosalynde whispered a silent prayer of thanks to the Goddess.

Giles helped her onto his saddle, then promptly mounted behind her, scooting as far back as he could possibly go. Perversely, the effort he took to avoid her amused Rosalynde, and she took some small comfort in the fact that he must still think her hideous.

For his part, Wilhelm scarcely ever dared look at her, and he seemed intensely aggravated by their current obligations. She was coming to see him as a sour-faced lout, who was saved from being handsome by the perpetual look of contempt he wore. If only he wouldn't frown so much, he might be as comely as his brother—which only brought her to wonder how these two could possibly be related. They didn't look much alike. Both had dark eyes, but *Wilhelm's* hair was black and straight, cut in the Norman fashion, whilst Giles's hair was golden-blond, like the color of honey, with soft, loose curls that teased at his nape.

Truly, the man was beautiful, unnaturally so, and Rosalynde couldn't help herself—casting backward glances. He had lashes so dark and thick as to appear painted, like that of a Saracen's. But, no matter how exquisite his face might appear, he was saved from prettiness by the firm lines of a very masculine jaw, and the huskiness of his male form.

In a flight of fancy, she dared imagine him her champion, in truth... and if he could change his surly attitude, perhaps Arwyn might like the brother.

Alas, she daren't contemplate why Seren didn't enter her vision at all. After all, Giles was her sister's intended, not hers. And yet... here they were... *together*... and Seren was nowhere to be found. It couldn't be a mere coincidence that out of all the horses in London, she had stolen the very one belonging to Giles de Vere, and here he was... without his given bride.

At any rate, it wasn't as though Seren could possibly love the man. Until yesterday, her sister had never even met him, and, regardless, Rose knew Seren well enough to know her heart. It could be that Seren herself had willed Giles to her rescue. Surely, far less fanciful tales had inspired bards' songs.

And yet, very clearly, her dubious savior did not share her fancy—not at the moment. All the while they rode, it seemed to Rose that he must be performing acrobatics to avoid her. Somehow, he'd managed to place his long arms about her, only bowed to such a degree that he wouldn't be forced to touch her. Sweet fates. If she only dared, she might have laughed.

On the other hand, her reaction to him was hardly amusing. It was... confusing...

With his arms embracing her and leaning so close, she caught scents of warm leather, sunshine and a heady muskiness that called to her woman's senses in a way she couldn't ignore. Trying to make sense of it all, she sat quietly, her back straight, her precious Book pressed to her breast, until, much to her dismay, they found the King's Road, abandoning the sanctuary of the woodlands, and the sight of the long, dusty lane, cleared of trees, gave her heart a flitter.

Once on the road, the canopy of green disappeared, the sky was clear for miles... the view entirely unobstructed to little black, beady eyes...

Rosalynde peered back over her shoulder. "My lord... do you not fear brigands might be watching the road?"

"Watching," he said with little concern. "But we have naught so much of value for the trouble it would cost them to take it."

And so, he might believe, but, in truth, they had something far, *far* more valuable than either of these men could ever imagine.

Rosalynde swallowed hard, despite the reassuring glimmer of the sword in his scabbard, and she made herself small, burrowing deeper into space between his arms, biting her tongue.

Anyone who looked upon the Book of Secrets might see only a well-used book of scripture, but the knowledge writ herein was old as time itself. And despite that there were many, many *grimoires* held across the realm, this was the only one penned by Taliesin, the father of their coven. On its face were marks that were no longer legible in their time, *magik* runes lost evermore, save by virtue of this one precious book.

Wilhelm suddenly gave his mare a gentle heel and moved ahead, saying, "I'd like to see *any* man *attempt* to relieve *me* of *my* valuables."

Surprised by the outburst, Rosalynde watched as his chest puffed, and he cast a glance over his shoulder, perhaps to gauge his brother's expression.

Behind her, Lord Giles offered a nearly inaudible grunt of frustration, but he said naught in response to his brother's boast. She sensed that Wilhelm was more a burr in his saddle—or, more to the occasion, a plain-faced nun he couldn't be rid of, and so he tolerated her. But though, in truth, Wilhelm was the larger man, she had a sense that Giles de Vere was no man to be trifled with, and she only wondered why the brother didn't fear him.

Then again, Rosalynde didn't fear her sisters either—not Elspeth nor Rhi, and most certainly not Arwyn or Seren. However, none of her sisters expected obeisance, even though Elspeth liked to control every aspect of every situation. And regardless, for all that they'd lived five girls to a crude little cottage, with no mother or father, they'd rarely ever fought, save for the occasional squabble over chores. They'd depended too much on each other, and it had taken every bit of their wit and energy to endure life at the priory.

It was incredible what could be accomplished altogether and how difficult life could be alone. But this, too, was a manifestation of the *hud*—the unity of spirit and the power of shared prayer. Even now, Rosalynde could *feel* her sisters' love. They were her strength in this mad, mad world, and she didn't know what she would do without them. Perhaps these two brothers simply needed a reason to look beyond their petty quarrels, and her mother would surely give it to them if she ever found them.

Sadly, if Rosalynde hoped to find herself relieved by their company, the longer they traveled together, the more agitated she became, and the more she missed her sweet sisters... the more she worried about her *glamour*.

And yet, so long as Giles de Vere kept pushing her away—gently, of course—she shouldn't worry about the spell.

Bored and ill at ease in perfect view of the heavens, Rosalynde longed for friendly conversation. "So, then... you are lord of Warkworth?" she asked.

"Earl," interjected the brother. He had been silent until this point, and it seemed to Rose that he'd been waiting for an opportunity to pounce.

"Appointed yesterday," said Giles, though he left it at that, making Rosalynde all the more curious. And yet, shouldn't that be something marvelous to crow about?

Clearly, the news didn't please the brother, and there must be a bit of the devil in Rosalynde, because she couldn't let it go—particularly since Lord Giles seemed so ready to shove her away every time she sought the sanctuary of his coat. "What a wonderful boon," she said.

"So it is."

"So, then, my lord, you must expound... what great deed have you performed to earn such a prestigious title? Did you perchance manage to save our king from his cousin... again?"

Wilhelm snickered, but, alas, if there was a note of

sarcasm in Rosalynde's tone, she didn't bother to regret it. *Everybody* knew there were an unseemly number of newly appointed earls during Stephen's reign, and he had, indeed, named a few of them for having saved him from Matilda. That thought amused her, though she hardly anticipated the answer he gave her. "I lived, whilst my father died," he said a little bitterly, and Rosalynde frowned.

"Oh," she said, deflated. "Pardon, my lord."

"Worry not," he said curtly, putting a hand to her back and pushing her gently forward.

Rosalynde frowned, annoyed.

It didn't make sense that her given champion should utterly abhor her, but perhaps it was unreasonable to think he might see beyond her *glamour*, especially since she didn't want him to. "Well, my lord... I hope you find peace in God."

"Thank you, Sister," he said, and fell again into a narrow silence—a quietude that neither brother gave any indication of wishing to end.

Ah, well... at least boredom wouldn't be the death of her...

Her mother might be, though considering that Giles was here, without Seren, something must have happened in London to waylay the hateful witch.

Conceivably, there *was* one person she could ask, but how could she broach the subject when she shouldn't even have any knowledge that Giles was supposed to wed her sister?

Oh, what a tangle...

11

If twenty times the girl had leaned back against him, twenty times Giles pushed her away. The bitter truth was that she wasn't very attractive, and so much as he didn't wish to be attracted to a nun, neither did he care to feel this particular nun's soft curves against his well-worn leathers.

And, don't think he hadn't noticed how much she wiggled—probably equally as annoyed by the material of her crude gown as Giles was by her proximity.

Forsooth, as cold as it was, he wondered irately why she did not wear the cloak Wilhelm discovered in his satchel, instead of trying to burrow into his. Though he didn't recognize the breed of animal, hers was rimmed with soft, black fur, and it would surely keep her warmer than Giles had a mind to.

What a mystery, she was, traveling with more gold than his brother earned in a given year, and wearing clothes that would have chafed his own skin raw, when she owned a cloak that could easily have passed as fashionable in Stephen's court. There was something about her... something that struck him as odd.

Despite her lack of sophistication, he believed she could be a lady, in truth—mayhap the spoiled daughter of a Welsh lord. Her accent was faint, but he recognized it just the same, and she wore a certain gleam in her eye... one he'd met in too many dissenters, and so much as her spirit did appeal to him... her face did not.

She wiggled backward, yet again, nestling her firm little backside too intimately into the crook of his thighs, and there it was again—a snicker—Giles frowned.

To his utter dismay, his body hadn't the first clue his brain must be disgusted by the woman seated before him.

His mutinous cock betrayed him, stirring, if only slightly, and he scooted back, again, this time as far as he could manage and still remain in the saddle. Any further, and he would be seated on the mare's rump.

In answer, the girl leaned again, this time resting her head on his shoulder and Giles frowned. "Have you grown weary of traveling already, Sister Rosalynde?"

"Oh, nay, my lord," she said, sweet as honey—not at all in keeping with her appearance. And nevertheless, with her back to him, he could almost imagine her to be... well, more like he'd imagined her to be when he'd first laid eyes upon her sleeping in the thicket. And regardless, there was too much glee in her tone... as though she enjoyed baiting him.

But why? If, in truth, she'd somehow gleaned his feelings about her appearance, she should be rightfully offended—unlike his nose.

Bloody hell.

Her hair smelled of... roses.

And while there was nothing quite so extraordinary about a Rose smelling like a rose—still, he frowned, wishing he could, at least for the time being, forget the girl's unpleasant face.

Sweet lord, he didn't wish to lean into that intoxicating scent... and neither did he appreciate her dark, shining hair spilling over his shoulder so familiarly as a lover's. Warmed by the noonday sun, it shone like red velvet.

Moreover, there was something about Sister Rosalynde that reminded him of the siren from his dreams... that beauteous water nymph that time after time had lured him to the depths of the sea. She'd had a similar gleam in her eyes that hardened his cock so painfully he awoke in the mornings with a burning desire that would not diminish until he took himself into his own hands. As soon as he found a moment alone, he must indulge himself again, as he didn't consider it to be in anybody's best interest for a man to burn.

"You seem to be very much at ease," he said, this time allowing her rest.

"Aye, my lord. Because, after all, you've been so kind." He caught a smile in her voice, and, inexplicably, it made his cock stir again. She inhaled deeply, her ample breasts brushing against his arm, and he shuddered over the sensation. "I was lost until you found me."

"Ah, yeah," he rejoined, perhaps testing her. "And what man, having a hundred sheep, if he has lost one, does not leave the ninety, to go after the one..."

"Ninety-nine," she said.

"Ninety-nine," he amended. "You do know your scripture, Sister Rosalynde."

She was silent a moment. "Alas, not so well as I should. But you also know yours?"

"I do, indeed," said Giles. "Until recently, I was...

conscripted to..." He peered at Wilhelm, who seemed to be doing his utmost to ignore them. "The seminary."

"I see," she said.

He very much doubted she did, and yet what he did and where he'd been until the day he'd returned to England was not a matter for public consumption. He cast a glance at his moody brother. Even despite their recent discussion, something was bedeviling Wilhelm, though Giles couldn't put a finger on it. He was tired, that much he could see. He was beginning to slouch in his saddle, but as tired as Giles might be, himself, he didn't intend to stop until Wilhelm begged for mercy. If he had to hand the nun over to keep him awake, he would do it—except... for some odd reason, he realized he didn't want to. And, more, the longer she remained burrowed in his arms, the stronger his desire to pull her back against him and keep her safe. The scent of her was like some witchery... lulling him into a state of bliss, making him long for his siren, invented though she must be.

"My lord, we've been traveling the King's Road for some time. Perhaps we should return to the woods?"

Sister Rosalynde peered over her shoulder yet again, and Giles cringed at the presentation of her face so near. It wasn't so much that she was unattractive, but to look at her made him feel drunk, and it didn't help much that he was already exhausted and growing more so by the second. He hadn't slept all night long. And so much as he didn't regret it, because of the return of his sable, he was growing more and more vexed by the mile—both at this sweet, unsuspecting nun, and his lame-brained, ill-tempered brother.

"We'll be fine," he reassured her, and hating himself for the rudeness, he gave her a twirling motion with his finger, so she would turn back around. If he must be forced to suffer the tantalizing curves of her body, he'd rather suffer his own imagination. But, if only... because she was perfectly formed. So much as he didn't wish to know that, he did, and it was impossible to deny it—as impossible to ignore as her sweet, beguiling scent, and he blamed it on his wasted state.

Consequently, the more confused he grew, the more cantankerous he became. "Sister, please, must you lean... so... close?"

Beside him, his brother chuckled, and Giles tensed.

Clearly, Wilhelm was enjoying his discomfort, and, evidently, he'd forgotten everything they'd discussed back in that tavern, else none of it had meant a bloody thing to him. It was enough to sour his mood.

"Say Wilhelm... do you recall my suggesting we stop by Neasham?"

"Of course," Wilhelm said, impatiently. "You said we could deliver Sister Rosalynde with time to spare."

"Nay, brother... before that... in the tavern... do you not recall I said we should stop to give alms for Lady Ayleth's soul?"

His brother did not answer—not at once, and when he did, his voice was thick with emotion. "Nay," he said. "I did not."

12

L*ady Ayleth?*
 Who was this woman who'd aroused such raw emotion betwixt these brothers?

Instinctively, she sensed Lady Ayleth must be the needle beneath their bums, the cause of their enmity, the pebble in their boots. But whoever she was, she must also be quite dead—or dying—since Rosalynde didn't believe one gave alms for the souls of the living.

Alms, as well as she could glean, were paid by the devout for the souls in purgatory, so they might be freed to see the pearly gates of Heaven. However, according to her own beliefs, there was only this world and the Other World. And, if, indeed, there was a third place, according to *dewine* tradition, it wasn't a place mortals could bargain their way out of.

The Nether Realm was a great black void where all things simply ceased to be, just as the Isle of Avalon and the Great Witch Cerridwen. It was as mysterious a place, even to a *dewine*, as the fae glens.

And yet, whatever the case, her heart ached for these brothers, even as she suffered a strange pang that could only be described as envy. Oh, to have a man love her so deeply that he would vie with his brother, even beyond her death. She sighed wistfully.

As a girl, she'd so much loved all those troubadours' songs. Every so often, as she and her sisters had toiled in their garden, bored and forgotten, she had dreamt of a beautiful champion who would ride to her rescue. In her dreams— she peered over her shoulder —he looked like Giles.

So, then, could this Lady Ayleth be the reason Giles de Vere had abandoned her beauteous sister in London?

Sad to say, if sweet, beautiful Seren did not manage to turn this man's heart or soften the pain of his loss, what hope had Rose to do the same? And why in the name of the Goddess would she aspire to do so? Had she gone mad?

Two days alone without her sisters and already she was pining over a man.

And regardless, she rebuked herself, simply because Elspeth had married her champion did not mean Rosalynde should do the same—nor was it even clear yet that Giles was any sort of champion at all. The man was a newly appointed earl to England's Usurper, and he might never dare risk his new title for the likes of Rosalynde, nor even Seren, for that matter.

And here was the plain truth: Rose was bound for Aldergh and her sister's husband was an enemy to the crown.

She was *not* some plain, hapless nun; she was a daughter of Avalon, a child of the Goddess. And just as soon as this came to be known, Giles de Vere would return her to her mother. Because if he so much as dared to oppose his king, he would sooner find himself dispossessed and perhaps even imprisoned.

As for Rosalynde... well... she would do well

enough to put all her romantic notions aside—forget the bards' tales, forget notions of courtly love and champions.

This was not the time for fantasies, and there was too much at stake here—war games, *politiks*, deception, brothers at odds—the realm was in peril. And if there was one thing she *must* accept, it was that Elspeth was right. She might not share Elspeth's love for *politiks*, nor any true affection for Matilda, but she now understood what a precarious path they were traveling as a nation, and if Matilda did not reclaim their father's throne, England might be lost.

For all these many months in London, Rosalynde had been so preoccupied with her own troubles that she hadn't had much of an inkling what was happening elsewhere in the realm. To her mind, there were only two places of consequence—Blackwood, where she believed Rhi was being held, and Aldergh, where her sister Elspeth had gone. Unlike Elspeth, she hadn't much interest to know about the Empress Matilda, what she was doing, who was whispering in her ear, or where she was going. Alas, she and her *true* sisters had more immediate concerns, and despite that she shared blood ties with Henry's daughter, Rosalynde could scarcely even recall Henry, much less a distant half-sister.

Now, in the fourteenth winter since Henry's death, why should she bother to care about a sister who was twenty-seven years her senior, and who'd never once troubled herself over their welfare?

Quite certainly, Matilda didn't care about them, and, for all that Elspeth seemed to admire the lady, she mustn't care about Elspeth either.

And yet why should she?

Their father had sired many, many bastards, and

despite that Matilda had loved Robert of Gloucester, it was probably because they were more of an age. She and Matilda were not, and they scarcely knew of each other. When Matilda left England to be married at the age of twelve, Rosalynde wasn't even born yet. When she returned to court after her husband died, Elspeth herself was but two. Three years later, when she'd married Geoffrey d' Anjou, even then, Rosalynde and Arwyn were scarce seedlings in their mother's womb.

Half a lifetime had already passed for Matilda by the time Rosalynde and Arwyn came wailing into the world. And, for those few times their half-sister had paid attendance to their father in London after their birth, she could scarce have been asked to bother with Morwen's brats. In her shoes, Rosalynde wouldn't have either. Not only was Morwen Henry Beauchamp's whore—a woman who'd disrespected her mother's memory—but even then, Matilda and Morwen had been at odds.

None of that mattered here and now. What did matter was her real sisters, and no man should come between them.

And anyway, she didn't even know for sure that Giles had repudiated Seren. For all Rosalynde knew, it simply hadn't been appropriate for him to bring her home—and here she sat pining over a man who didn't even know her true face.

How ludicrous was that?

Perhaps, after all, Giles was looking forward to wedding her sister... and mayhap Seren, too, had found him appealing. Who wouldn't? Only now, Rosalynde was behaving like a wanton, prepared to throw herself into his arms—and why? Because she had some silly notion that the Goddess may have deigned to send her a champion... as she had for Elspeth?

This was hardly a fae's tale. Lives were at stake, and hers no less than anyone else's. She hoped, in truth, that the Goddess had been gracious enough to send her a champion, but it mustn't be for flights of fancy. She had her mother's *grimoire* in her possession, and if she didn't keep her wits about her, she would lose it, and lose her life, as well.

Moreover, if she wasn't careful, she would send these brothers to their deaths, as well.

That was a sobering thought.

Brooding now, she held the *grimoire* close, trying to remember what she knew of Giles de Vere—not much.

He was a younger son, come into his inheritance after the death of his sire and an elder brother. Morwen had had little more to say about the man, but Rosalynde had never sensed that her mother wished to give Seren up so easily—not to some lowly northern lord, who hadn't any true power or influence. In fact, she'd had the impression that Morwen was furious over the betrothal and that she might thwart the king if she could. Perhaps, after all, that's what waylaid her? Perhaps she'd angered Stephen and he had locked her away, as his wife so oft threatened to do.

To be sure, the Queen Consort was no wilting flower. As diminutive as the lady might be, she swept through Westminster's halls with a stature that cowed men twice her size. Nor did she concern herself with niceties. The one time the sisters had been left alone in her company, she'd informed them rather baldly that her mother should be *persona non grata*, and that the only reason she was not, was because of her. Simply because Morwen was useful, the Queen would continue to pave the way for the Pendragons in her court, but if a one of them crossed her, they would see how fast they would be put out the door.

Rosalynde also remembered Elspeth telling a story about the day they were summoned to meet Stephen for the first time—right after his coronation. Rosalynde was far too young to remember the occasion, but apparently, the Queen had marched into their mother's quarters and informed Morwen in no uncertain terms to be discreet with her lord king, lest she defy her husband and feed Morwen's eyeballs to her precious birds.

No one spoke to Morwen that way. *No one.* But, after all, there must be something dark in Stephen's queen, because what sort of wife conspired with a husband's paramour? What sort of mother encouraged a son—England's heir—to disport where her husband had already dared?

In Rosalynde's opinion, if, in truth, England fell to ruin, the fault would lie as much with Maude as it did with Morwen.

But, for all that he'd stolen her father's crown, Stephen seemed more reasonable. Certainly, he was kinder, and Rosalynde had a niggling sense that he was a man caught in a spider's web, and his queen was as much a poppet master as her mother. Alas, she also sensed the king was growing weary of his throne. Rumor had it that he was preparing to abdicate to his son—completely unheard of in England, though they often did such things in France—and if he did, Morwen and Stephen's Queen would gnash their teeth like wolves, and God help Eustace, the poor, arrogant fool. He was too stupid, greedy, shortsighted and godless to survive them. They would rend him in two like a rag doll.

The thought gave Rosalynde a shiver, and she shivered again, feeling the first signs of cold. And not merely the cold...

It was all she could do to keep her head from lolling and her eyes wide open. In her current state, she doubted she would have any recourse against her mother. She would lie down at Morwen's feet and snore herself into an early grave.

Gooseflesh erupted on her skin as Giles slid an arm about her waist, pulling her close, lending his warmth and his support. This time her shivers had naught do with the weather.

"Rest," he said. "We'll stop soon."

The tenderness in his voice startled her, and the warmth of his breath against her nape made her heart flutter wildly. She said not a word—couldn't speak, because now the tightness of her throat strangled her words. But she nodded, shivering as she laid her head back to rest against his shoulder.

Goddess have mercy, despite having spent the past hour talking herself out of girlish fancies, she dared to revel in the warmth and safety of his arms.

S he was in a castle that could only be Blackwood.

Born in London, neither Rosalynde nor Arwyn had ever chanced to see their family estate in Bannau Brycheiniog, but she recalled every word of Elspeth's stories, and she envisioned it clearly... the ivy-tangled courtyard with the sacred cauldron once tended by Gwion, that boy who'd stolen the Witch Goddess's potion. Pregnant still, and fat with its great iron belly, the cauldron sat above a ring of blackened stones, the fire beneath it burning with an eternal flame. Rose couldn't see what was being brewed within, but she watched smoke that curled above the cauldron and rose into the open courtyard toward a cloudless blue sky, rushing past lichen-covered stone...

And then, suddenly, she herself was the smoke... drifting through rusted metal bars and coalescing into a solid form...

Here, from her prison bower, she had a view of the Endless Sea... and outside her door stood a man... leaning against the wall, facing away, so she couldn't see his face, though she could still hear his voice. "There is no future but the one your mother has ordained."

Familiar laughter. "Ah, my lord... the Goddess truly

works in mysterious ways. You have yet to realize what you would give to win your true desire."

Silence.

"And what if my desire is you?"

Like wisps of smoke from the cauldron, her lips curved into a slow smile, and she laughed again, very softly, even as her nipples hardened with desire. "And you jest, my lord... but you will learn... the heart wants what it wants."

Silence.

"No matter what you may call yourself, your blood is Welsh, lest you forget... and I know what you really want."

She was not afraid, though his words should engender fear. "You will never leave here... Rhiannon," he said, angry, and then she heard him push off the wall and walk away.

His footsteps echoed sharply on the ancient stone.

Silence was the gift of his departure.

Rhiannon!

Rosalynde's eyes flew wide to find it was late afternoon.

She was horrified to discover herself resting like a limp doll in Giles's arms. Straightening at once, embarrassed, she saw that he'd laid a hand atop her *grimoire*, holding it fast, and without meaning to, Rosalynde wrenched the Book away with a gasp.

"Pardon," he said. "I feared you would drop it and I didn't wish to wake you."

Disoriented still, Rosalynde jerked forward, trying to gauge how far they'd come. As far as she could tell, they were still alive... and still on the King's Road.

On the road, their ambling shadows formed gargoyles—two of them: one big one small—with hoofed protuberances pawing at the ground, and thick bodies with strange appendages growing from their middles, five jouncing heads. For a befuddled instant, she studied the grotesque shadows, realizing that Wilhelm must have fallen behind, and she turned to find him hunched over his horse, somehow dozing. "How long have I been sleeping?" she asked.

"A bit longer than Wilhelm."

Rose tilted her head, stretching the cords of her neck, and turned again to peer at Wilhelm, marveling over the contortion of his body and his curious ability to sleep in his saddle. At least she'd had Giles to hold her, and for that she was thankful. And nevertheless, she was horrified to discover that, like Rhiannon's had in her dream, her nipples were pebbled and straining against the course wool of her nun's habit. Defensively, she pressed the *grimoire* closer.

Ignoring her traitorous body, she considered the dream. Could it be that her sister had given her a glimpse into her cage? Or, was it only an invention of Rosalynde's tired, overwrought mind?

Some *dewines* could descry by dreams—Rhiannon did so all the time, but Rosalynde had never once had any occurrence herself, and she only knew it because Rhiannon had told her so, not because her sister had ever infiltrated her dreams before. And yet, no *dewine* worth her blood would ever ignore a message from the *aether*, and it was quite possible Rhiannon had discovered a safer way to *mindspeak*.

"I'm guessing you mustn't have rested well last night," Giles said. "Much to be expected, there aren't many ladies I know who could sleep so well in the woods."

Clearly, he didn't know her. Rosalynde could sleep anywhere, and the forest was like a second home to her.

Once, she'd fallen asleep in an elm tree, like a cat, and her sisters had worried all day long until she'd returned to the priory that evening. Even so, she was chagrined to confess, even if only to herself, that she had rested far more easily in Giles's arms than she had in her warded pentacle.

"Speaking of woods, my lord..." She peered up, looking at clear skies—completely unobstructed by the boughs of trees, in perfect view of Morwen's black-feathered spies. "Should we not seek the shade for a while?"

She turned to look at him with pleading eyes.

GILES BLINKED at the sight of her very, very blue eyes... but he'd imagined they were green—a shade of green that recalled him to rich, thick moss, not this peculiar shade of blue that made him think of bellflowers.

"What is it?" she asked.

Giles scratched his chin, uncertain what *it* was, precisely.

"My lord?" She asked again, and he shook his head, averting his gaze, suffering the same bewildering sense of recognition he'd experienced this morning when he'd met her.

"'Tis naught," he said, determining that he must be over-weary.

So long as she'd been sleeping, he'd let her rest because he'd wanted to put as much distance between them and Darkwood as possible. He didn't care to alarm the girl, but he had a sense they were being followed, even despite that he couldn't see anyone. It was entirely possible they'd caught the attention of one of Darkwood's brigands, and the man was skilled enough to know how to track them, and perhaps wise enough to know that he couldn't prevail against two armed warriors—which also implied he must be alone, perhaps waiting for an opportune moment.

He hadn't bothered alerting Wilhelm only because his sword lay resting as quietly as the woman in his arms. Regretfully, stopping for the evening was inevitable and now was as good a time as any. He was the only one who hadn't managed to catch a kip in the saddle.

And, anyway, he'd already proven his point. Wilhelm had been dozing nearly as long as Rosalynde, and if he denied it, Giles had the girl as his witness. Clearly, his brother had judged himself in superior form. Alas, he was merely the bigger man. And, regardless, it annoyed Giles to no end that this unlooked-for competition had reduced him to a youth, fresh off the field, with balls bigger than his brains, and a yen to prove himself where he oughtn't bloody care to.

Sister Rosalynde was still looking at him, pleading, and he gave a short whistle, heard a waking snort, then an immediate shift in Wilhelm's gait. Without turning, he waved his brother into the woods, where the late afternoon sun sluiced through the limbs of naked oaks.

He found a spot near a small burn, where he could see clearly in three directions, and there he dismounted, then helped Sister Rosalynde down from his horse, making sure she was steady on her feet before releasing her...

Blue.

Her eyes were, indeed, blue. Bright as bellflowers.

And more... under the soft, dappled light of the forest, she appeared... different.

Softer, perhaps?

Peering up, over the dingy white veil she wore, her

lovely blue eyes were filled with concern, and she held the book between them like a shield.

Amused, Giles released her, and gave the book a nod. "There's room in my satchel," he suggested. "Along with your cloak..."

"Nay, thank you," she said quickly, casting a glance at the sword in his scabbard, the shining rain guard catching her attention as it glinted by the sun. She gasped suddenly, gave a hasty pardon and hurried away, giving him the impression that his sword had intimidated her.

Shrugging, he watched her go, wondering again why she wouldn't wear her cloak. Clearly, she was cold, or she wouldn't have been so insistent about climbing beneath his own, and yet...

He had a feeling there was more to Sister Rosalynde than what she'd claimed... and despite her outward appearance, there was something about the lady that appealed to him. There was a spark of brilliance behind those chameleon eyes.

"Do not wander," he called after her. "Hurry back, or I'll come looking."

14

Not only could Giles not be sure they weren't alone in these woods, but his brother was in a fine state to be hunting. Suffering the effects of too much ale and too little sleep, Wilhelm was cantankerous and restless, and Giles didn't intend for Sister Rosalynde to be mistaken for quarry whilst kneeling behind a bush. He gave her plenty long enough to see to her affairs, before he went searching, sword in hand.

He'd found her repairing the hem of her gown, but she'd complained fiercely when he'd insisted that she return. Now she sat, pouting and worrying her hands raw as Giles finished gathering kindling for the fire.

But it struck him, as he watched her, that for all her worrying, she didn't appear overly concerned about Giles, nor about Wilhelm for that matter—a man thrice her size. She was barely constraining her temper, and the look in her eyes reminded him of a cornered wolf—wary and desperate, quite prepared to bite the hand feeding her.

He also had a very strong sense that, despite her weariness, she didn't wish to stop for the evening, and he recalled how nervous she'd been about staying on the King's Road, in perfect view of fellow travelers.

Perhaps she knew something about the man who was following them?

Perhaps she was running from a husband, or a father?

Whatever the case, the more time he spent with *Sister Rosalynde*, the more certain he was that she wasn't who she claimed to be. He'd known many women in service to God, and for what it was worth, she didn't appear to him to be any sort of candidate for the veil.

He gave her a patient smile as he adjusted the kindling and gave it another click of his fire-steel, annoyed that he hadn't been able to find more suitable wood. "If you must return, I would happily escort you."

"Nay," she said, peevishly. And then, with a tilt of her head, she asked, "Did no one ever teach you that ladies must have privacy? We do not brandish our... *swords*... in public, as men are wont to do."

Giles choked on his laughter.

It wasn't immediately clear which *sword* she'd intended as her meaning. But, either way, it was clearly a rebuke.

God help her sisters at Neasham—and then, a thought occurred to him: Perhaps, with her five gold marks, she'd intended to bribe her way into the nunnery. Only now that her money was gone, she would have one hell of a time convincing the prioress to take on another mouth to feed—particularly one so colorful as hers.

Nevertheless, she clearly prized her scripture. She hadn't let that bloody book out of her sight since the moment he'd laid eyes upon her.

And regardless, with that impudent lift of her chin, she would be wasted in a priory. She was spirited, strong and bright. And while, in truth, her face might not be so exquisite as his intended's, the more he looked at her... the more he recognized a certain quality that spoke to his heart.

There was an inner light that shone from Sister Rosalynde's eyes. Even with her odd face and penchant for the veil, he would prefer this woman any day over Seren Pendragon.

But Seren Pendragon was the least of his concerns, and so, too, should be this mouthy nun. He had more urgent matters to settle... not the least of which was the disenfranchising of a king and his idiot son. The Count of Mortain was swiftly becoming a scourge to England. He was dangerous, petty and reckless, and if he continued, unmanaged, he would plunge the entire nation into hell itself. What was more, Morwen Pendragon would be the fallen angel who would usher them in. And this was *not* puffery, nor a disgruntled lord speaking... nor a man who'd lost his kindred to an idiot's rampage.

If any other man had done half what Eustace had purportedly done, undermining what little of his father's good will remained, he would have been drawn and quartered. Instead, the mouthy bugger beat his hairless chest even as he laid waste to England, taxing loyal lords, until even those who'd willingly supported his father now begged to see Duke Henry reclaim England's throne—and so he would.

So he would.

In the meantime, Giles wanted naught more than to take his new title—and his lovely betrothed—and shove them both up Stephen's arse. Beautiful as the lady might be, her mother would stop at naught to see her will done. And Giles knew as well as Wilhelm that it was by her counsel that Eustace had burned Warkworth to the ground. Still, even knowing this, he'd stood in Stephen's hall, watching those complicit fools twitter like birds into each other's ears, and it was all he could do not to unsheathe his sword, there and then, and climb the stairs to the dais to claim their heads.

Alas, he could not so easily have wiped the smug smile off Morwen Pendragon's face without sacrificing his own life and Wilhelm's as well.

Or, for that matter, putting *everything* at risk.

But now he had another axe to bear for Wilhelm's sake. After everything his brother had endured, he had been forced to stand by Giles's side and watch as they'd awarded him an earldom—inexplicably—whilst neither their father nor Roger ever achieved the honor—and, no less, in the presence of Morwen Pendragon. Giles would like to gut them all, if only for pouring fuel over the fire of Wilhelm's rage. His once good-natured bother was no longer the gladsome fool. The Wilhelm he'd known was dead... perished the night of the fire. He was now pettish and brooding, and as tiresome as it was becoming, Giles was determined to endure it with patience. He only wished he could tell the bloody fool that vengeance was forthcoming. But, all in good time, for the Church itself had an investment in Stephen's ruin.

"My lord?"

Giles couldn't say he'd forgotten she was there—not precisely—though he'd made it a point not to look at her again. More and more, he was growing ambivalent to her presence, inexplicably drawn to the lady even though she was not at all his type. And even if she were—Good Christ, she was a nun, a woman of the cloth. It was quite unsettling to feel his cock stir in her presence—and more so over the petting of her stupid book.

"Are *we* truly to kindle a fire?"

There was disapproval in her tone, and perhaps a bit of ire. Giles clicked the fire-steel a few more times, annoyed that the wood was so green and wet. "Aye," he said. "*I* am." And he cast her a brief glance, fighting anew his desire to stare. *That face...* every time he looked at her, he felt as though he had tippled too many ales.

"My lord... 'tis daylight yet. Shouldn't we press on?"

Something in her tone gave him pause, and he turned to look at her, considering...

ROSALYNDE HAD CAUGHT a brief glimpse of herself in the perfectly polished rain guard of his sword. Her true countenance was returning, but he didn't allow her any time to retrieve her philter, much less see to her spell.

He stared now with narrowed black eyes, his dark gaze probing, and she felt his regard as surely as she felt the change coming over her.

Already, her face felt woolly, and the sensation seemed to be spreading. Moreover, the splotches on her hands appeared to be shifting. Rubbing them vigorously, she hoped to delay the change by sheer will alone.

Breathe, she commanded herself.

Breathe, Rose.

With every second that passed, she grew more acutely aware of the needle and *philter* in her hem and her immense desire to retrieve them.

"We've pushed the horses enough for one day," he said finally, returning his attention to his kindling—arranging it too meticulously, if you asked Rose.

Sweet fates, had he noticed something awry?

Nay, Rose, nay! Calm yourself. All is well, she reassured. *Only think...*

Morwen didn't appear to have to recast her *glamour* daily, therefore it mustn't be necessary—unless... there was something Morwen was adding to her *philter...* something Rosalynde and her sisters had overlooked.

Impressions of Darkwood assaulted her, and she shuddered to think what added ingredient her mother might have included. Forcing those memories out of her head, she watched as Giles struck his fire-steel to the damp wood—over and over again, until the sound of it grated on her nerves.

He frowned then, and rose to search for more kindling, and meanwhile Rose tried to calm herself.

Truly, there could be *no* true change. The *glamour* wasn't even real. It was only a chimera, a spirit mask, a suggestion from the Goddess to deceive mortal eyes. Insofar as she knew, only blood *magik* could ever truly alter flesh—ergo perhaps the one who'd cast the *glamour* could always see beyond the countenance it revealed to others? Surely, if her face had changed so much, he would be demanding answers—and regardless, she was still wearing her wimple and veil.

And yet, even if her glamour was still working, there was another problem she hadn't foreseen: How was she going toward the camp tonight? It simply wouldn't be possible to do so with these men as her witnesses.

Nay, she couldn't stay here, waiting to be discovered. She had to go. *Now*. Before it was too late. She had a terrible, terrible sense of impending doom... like a storm cloud descending.

"Well," she said, when Giles returned. "I was desperately hoping to arrive at Neasham soon."

He turned to look at her again, then averted his eyes. *Sweet Goddess* every time he tore his gaze away, she expelled a breath she'd not realized she'd held. "And you will," he said. "But not tonight. Even with strong coursers, we're a week or more away."

One week!

Rosalynde answered him with silence, though perhaps he could feel her disappointment hanging in the air, for he asked, without turning, "Art expected, Sister?"

"Nay, oh, nay..." She slid a hand beneath her veil to touch her burning cheek. "Not precisely."

Already, everything was becoming impossible, and she was growing weary of the lies. For all she knew, this was how her mother's malevolence had begun, with small lies at first, then big lies, until her entire life became a frightening deception.

She lifted her hand from her cheek to her forehead, pressing it firmly across her very warm face, dismayed and confused, hoping the gesture might still the tempest in her head.

Goddess please...

Here she was, seated atop a stump, like a bloody toad on a pad, waiting to be devoured by... what? What sort of beast gobbled toads? It didn't matter, and regardless, Rosalynde was quite certain the poor toad would have been seated as she was right now... feeling this crippling sense of doom, only too bewildered to move. After all, this was something *all* mortals shared in common—a keen sense of intuition, and a strong desire to deny it. She was beside herself with worry now, her thoughts spinning nightmarish yarns.

And this man... would he run screaming if he learned who and what she was?

Rosalynde cast a worried glance at her dubious savior. He was still kneeling by his unwilling fire, and so much as she didn't wish him to succeed, the clicking of his fire-steel was grating on her delicate nerves.

Finally, when she grew tired of watching and listening to him spark the fire-steel to the damp wood without success, she narrowed her gaze over the pile of tinder and summoned the essence of fire.

Unseen ribbons gathered the sun's waning light, focusing its heat into a small point of light.

Rosalynde's *dewine* eyes could see what he could not see—the twisting and turning of the *aether* as her flame leapt to life, even before he could strike his fire-steel to the tinder one more time.

He froze, staring at his stack of wood with what appeared to be a mixture of surprise and confusion and Rosalynde regretted her impetuousness at once.

"How resourceful you are," she said, wincing, because at the instant, she was becoming her own worst enemy.

She was only tired, she reassured herself, but huffed a sigh, without realizing how dramatic she sounded—until Giles turned to look at her again.

"Is something troubling you, Sister?"

"Oh, nay... I am but missing my sisters." Thankfully, this was no lie. She missed her sisters more than words could say, particularly Arwyn. Her twin understood her better than anyone, and though they couldn't be more different, Arwyn was everything she

15

...was not possible.

...utside the door could be heard an occa-
...uffling of feet—guards, probably, but little
...r came from wandering the halls by night.
... nights ago, a woman had been murdered,
... left to be discovered by the palace guards.
...as dangerous as Westminster's halls might be,
...ght, with Mordecai still at large, both Seren
...yn were contemplating escape.

...s impossible to say what could be keeping

...by day, the king was growing over suspicious,
...g everyone was out to subvert him, particu-
...w that the Archbishop of Canterbury had
...tly refused to confirm his heir, leaving his suc-
...in question and reinforcing the illegitimacy of
...n. Rumors abounded that he had sent agents
... court to ferret out spies. Some were whis-
...ies to fill their purses. But, whatever the case—
...er had detained Morwen, there could be no
...hat when she returned, she would peel the
...m their bodies to attain what information she
...d. Both girls had recognized the look in her

was not, and she was everything Arwyn was not. Together they were whole.

"Your sisters... at Neasham?"

"Aye," said Rose, quickly, and Giles gave her another glance, though his gaze didn't linger.

"I rather had the impression you'd yet to join your
sisters at Neasham, and that you were bringing your
life's fortune."

"Well, so I was."

He turned to assess her, again with narrowed eyes.
"So, then, what is it you were doing in London?"

For the sake of her soul, Rose attempted to compromise one last lie, pretending a calm she couldn't
possibly feel. "I was there to retrieve my inheritance."

"But then you lost it... to your *guide*?"

She gave him a disapproving glance—not so different from what she'd imagine a mother might do to
a wayward son. "Nay, my lord. So difficult as it might
be for men to imagine, gold and silver are the least of
my earthly treasures." He narrowed his gaze on her
book and Rosalynde picked it up and put it in her lap.
"It belonged... to my grandmamau," she said.

He considered her another moment before he
asked, "Do I detect a bit of Welsh in your accent?"

Rosalynde forced a smile. "You have a good ear, my
lord. My mother was Welsh, my father... English. He's
dead now."

"And your mother?"

"Dead, as well." Or, she might as well be. In so
many ways Elspeth had been more of a mother to her
and her sisters than Morwen ever was. Morwen simply
couldn't be bothered with anyone who didn't serve her
immediate needs. Left to their own devices, she and her
four sisters had been forced to look after one another.

Of course, it was one thing to be born a legitimate heir to the crown, another to be a king's bastard. She supposed she should be thankful that they'd been allowed to wander the palace, until such time as they were no longer welcome... Once she and Arwyn turned six—the year their father died—she and her sisters were roused from their beds in the middle of the night and ferreted away to Llanthony in Wales, to be hidden away like embarrassments—or at least that's the way it seemed to Rosalynde.

Morwen always claimed that it was for their own good and she'd only meant to keep them safe from harm, but she'd spoken those words with the tenor of a lie. In retrospect, she'd only pretended to fear Stephen's wrath, and she'd claimed that he'd meant to dispose of Henry's children—illegitimate or nay—but from where Rosalynde stood now, that never appeared to be the case. Rather, it seemed to Rosalynde that the only thing Morwen was ever afraid of was that her five little brats would get in her way. She was despicable, and her years of neglect had left Rosalynde with an emptiness in her heart that might never be assuaged.

It was no wonder she was looking to Giles for... *what?*

Now that his fire was burning stronger, he surprised her by coming over and sitting beside her.

"It looks to be quite old. May I?" He lifted a hand as though to request Rosalynde's book, and then, when she didn't hand it over at once, he told her, "As I've said, I spent quite a few years in the seminary."

"It is old," she said. But still, she pressed the tome closer to her breast, protecting it, even though she didn't believe he could see what she saw. Regardless, she daren't allow him to have it. It was far, far too precious, and she didn't wish to let it out of her hands—

not even for an instant. ﹖ nor woman would ever ﹔ that was beginning to be ﹖ remained in this... this... protected, the more pro﹖ would do precisely that.

Her mother.

Morwen Pendragon.

A fallen daughter of Aval﹖

His hand remained t﹖ seeching...

"I beg pardon, my lord...

He gave her an odd glan﹖ an instant longer. Thankfull﹖ denying him again. Return﹖ hand, he grinned broadly as﹖ conies.

"Hungry?" he asked.

eyes as she'd walked out the door. It promised the worst of her *hud du.*

Neither Seren nor Arwyn were experienced *dewines*, and until that night at Darkwood, neither had truly understood what depravity could be wrought by *magik* of any sort, nor why good folks should fear them. But that night, they'd learned. And it soon became apparent that their mother was not to be bargained with. She reveled in their tears.

Resolved now—for what better chance would they have?— the girls moved swiftly through the chamber, gathering all the supplies they could carry. Every loose piece of silver and gold Morwen possessed—everything that was not locked away—they shoved into sacks. Then, they turned to more perishable items— anything they could find to sustain them.

With a bit of good fortune, they might find themselves reunited with Elspeth or Rhiannon.

Finally, when they were ready to walk out the door, Seren's gaze fell upon the scrying stone that had once belonged to their grandmamau.

It was too large to take in its current form. It would be impossible to travel with... and yet.

Rosalynde had the Book of Secrets, and here sat Merlin's Crystal. To leave it with Morwen was folly, because their mother would only use it to vanquish them—and more importantly, she would use it to find Rosalynde.

Seren herself had never witnessed its use, but they knew it was precious and powerful, and in its current state, their mother could easily use it to ferret them out.

Gently, Seren lifted up the scrying stone. The instant she touched it, the interior began to shift, the stone swirling and billowing through the marbled depths like a storm made of crystal. Helpless to do aught but watch, their eyes became affixed to the images forming...

Passed down through the ages, the scrying stone was powerful, indeed. As the story went, even as the Witch Goddess Cerridwen had been sucked into the depths of her watery prison, her screams had formed bubbles that drifted to the surface. The instant her breath returned to the *aether*, it solidified into crystals, the largest being the crystal Seren held in her hands— Merlin's Jewel. In the stone's opaque, vaguely shimmering depths, she saw lithe figures arising from mist... a man ... kneeling... and... Rosalynde, seated on a stump in her nun's habit. Her *glamour* was gone, and she was watching some man kindle his fire.

Arwyn gasped, sounding dismayed. "She has revealed herself," she said.

Seren tilted her head to continue watching. "Not necessarily... the crystal would naturally reveal her to us; it would never be fooled by her *glamour*."

"What should we do?"

The sun was rising, sending tendrils of soft pink in through their windows. Soon the palace would wake, with a great swell of breath, like a stone beast arising from slumber.

And soon... Morwen was bound to return.

Some part of Seren longed to ask the crystal where she might be, but both she and her sister were still beguiled by the images the crystal had revealed to them —Rosalynde... in the company of... was he her champion?

And then Seren looked closer... recognizing the man. "Sweet, merciful Goddess!"

"What is it, Seren?"

Seren's hand flew to her lips in wonder. "That, my dearest Arwyn, is Giles de Vere."

Arwyn's entire face screwed with confusion. "*Your* betrothed?"

"So it seems."

The sisters lifted their gazes to peer into one another's eyes, blinking in surprise. Why would Seren's betrothed be Rosalynde's champion? Could it be that he was acting in her mother's behalf? What were they doing together?

"Will she be alright?"

Seren's brows drew together and she shook her head, but she said, "He did not strike me as an evil man, but who can say, Arwyn. The Goddess works in mysterious ways."

"What should we do?"

"I don't know."

"Should we warn Rose?"

Seren inhaled a fortifying breath, though she still could not wrest her gaze away from the crystal. "Nay," she said. "We daren't risk it... not now. Instead, we must pray he was sent to aid her."

The sounds of people stirring resounded from the hall, doors opening, whispers filtering in under the crack beneath their door. "If we mean to, we must go now," urged Arwyn, peering nervously at the door.

At last, Seren lifted her gaze from the crystal. "What about the scrying stone?"

"We cannot leave it."

But it was too big to carry afoot. Morwen had a special leather pouch that hung over her pommel, but they would have no horse to carry it, and even now, it felt inordinately heavy in Seren's hands, because within its hallowed depths, it bore all the possibilities of the *aether*—all things to come, all things past, and all things that lingered in twilight.

For a long, long moment, the sisters stared at one another, their gazes shifting back and forth, one to another, and each to Merlin's Jewel, where Rosalynde and her dubious champion remained visible.

Giles de Vere had abandoned the woodpile, and moved to sit beside their sister, and Arwyn said softly, "Do it, Seren. The Goddess will forgive you."

Ancient and irreplaceable, there was no other scrying stone of its worth in the entire World. There were certainly others with less power, but this was the only crystal born of the breath of the dragon. Like the Book of Secrets, it was priceless. "Do it," Arwyn said, urging her.

Seren, gave her sister a nod of accord, and with one last glance at the door—lest Morwen enter and surprise them—and an inhale of breath for courage, she lifted her arms high and brought them crashing down, releasing the ancient stone to the floor. It shattered at their feet, exploding into a thousand shards, its vague sea-green glow at once diminished, like a flame extinguished.

At once, both girls bent to grab a small piece—if only for posterity—and then, shoving the pieces of Merlin's Jewel into their rucksacks, they left what remained on the floor, rushing to the door.

was not, and she was everything Arwyn was not. Together they were whole.

"Your sisters... at Neasham?"

"Aye," said Rose, quickly, and Giles gave her another glance, though his gaze didn't linger.

"I rather had the impression you'd yet to join your sisters at Neasham, and that you were bringing your life's fortune."

"Well, so I was."

He turned to assess her, again with narrowed eyes. "So, then, what is it you were doing in London?"

For the sake of her soul, Rose attempted to compromise one last lie, pretending a calm she couldn't possibly feel. "I was there to retrieve my inheritance."

"But then you lost it... to your *guide*?"

She gave him a disapproving glance—not so different from what she'd imagine a mother might do to a wayward son. "Nay, my lord. So difficult as it might be for men to imagine, gold and silver are the least of my earthly treasures." He narrowed his gaze on her book and Rosalynde picked it up and put it in her lap. "It belonged... to my grandmamau," she said.

He considered her another moment before he asked, "Do I detect a bit of Welsh in your accent?"

Rosalynde forced a smile. "You have a good ear, my lord. My mother was Welsh, my father... English. He's dead now."

"And your mother?"

"Dead, as well." Or, she might as well be. In so many ways Elspeth had been more of a mother to her and her sisters than Morwen ever was. Morwen simply couldn't be bothered with anyone who didn't serve her immediate needs. Left to their own devices, she and her four sisters had been forced to look after one another.

Of course, it was one thing to be born a legitimate heir to the crown, another to be a king's bastard. She supposed she should be thankful that they'd been allowed to wander the palace, until such time as they were no longer welcome... Once she and Arwyn turned six—the year their father died—she and her sisters were roused from their beds in the middle of the night and ferreted away to Llanthony in Wales, to be hidden away like embarrassments—or at least that's the way it seemed to Rosalynde.

Morwen always claimed that it was for their own good and she'd only meant to keep them safe from harm, but she'd spoken those words with the tenor of a lie. In retrospect, she'd only pretended to fear Stephen's wrath, and she'd claimed that he'd meant to dispose of Henry's children—illegitimate or nay—but from where Rosalynde stood now, that never appeared to be the case. Rather, it seemed to Rosalynde that the only thing Morwen was ever afraid of was that her five little brats would get in her way. She was despicable, and her years of neglect had left Rosalynde with an emptiness in her heart that might never be assuaged.

It was no wonder she was looking to Giles for... *what?*

Now that his fire was burning stronger, he surprised her by coming over and sitting beside her.

"It looks to be quite old. May I?" He lifted a hand as though to request Rosalynde's book, and then, when she didn't hand it over at once, he told her, "As I've said, I spent quite a few years in the seminary."

"It is old," she said. But still, she pressed the tome closer to her breast, protecting it, even though she didn't believe he could see what she saw. Regardless, she daren't allow him to have it. It was far, far too precious, and she didn't wish to let it out of her hands—

not even for an instant. So long as she lived, no man nor woman would ever pry it out of her hands—and that was beginning to be the dilemma. The longer she remained in this... this... place, undefended and un-protected, the more probable it was that someone would do precisely that.

Her mother.

Morwen Pendragon.

A fallen daughter of Avalon.

His hand remained turned between them, be-seeching...

"I beg pardon, my lord... I would prefer not."

He gave her an odd glance, his hand lingering only an instant longer. Thankfully, Wilhelm saved her from denying him again. Returning with their supper in hand, he grinned broadly as he held up two fair-sized conies.

"Hungry?" he asked.

S leep was not possible.

Outside the door could be heard an occasional shuffling of feet—guards, probably, but little good ever came from wandering the halls by night. Only two nights ago, a woman had been murdered, her body left to be discovered by the palace guards. And yet, as dangerous as Westminster's halls might be, by first light, with Mordecai still at large, both Seren and Arwyn were contemplating escape.

It was impossible to say what could be keeping Morwen.

Day by day, the king was growing over suspicious, believing everyone was out to subvert him, particularly now that the Archbishop of Canterbury had steadfastly refused to confirm his heir, leaving his succession in question and reinforcing the illegitimacy of his reign. Rumors abounded that he had sent agents into his court to ferret out spies. Some were whispering lies to fill their purses. But, whatever the case—whatever had detained Morwen, there could be no doubt that when she returned, she would peel the skin from their bodies to attain what information she required. Both girls had recognized the look in her eyes as she'd walked out the door. It promised the worst of her *hud du.*

Neither Seren nor Arwyn were experienced *dewines*, and until that night at Darkwood, neither had truly understood what depravity could be wrought by *magik* of any sort, nor why good folks should fear them. But that night, they'd learned. And it soon became apparent that their mother was not to be bargained with. She reveled in their tears.

Resolved now—for what better chance would they have?— the girls moved swiftly through the chamber, gathering all the supplies they could carry. Every loose piece of silver and gold Morwen possessed—everything that was not locked away—they shoved into sacks. Then, they turned to more perishable items—anything they could find to sustain them.

With a bit of good fortune, they might find themselves reunited with Elspeth or Rhiannon.

Finally, when they were ready to walk out the door, Seren's gaze fell upon the scrying stone that had once belonged to their grandmamau.

It was too large to take in its current form. It would be impossible to travel with... and yet.

Rosalynde had the Book of Secrets, and here sat Merlin's Crystal. To leave it with Morwen was folly, because their mother would only use it to vanquish them—and more importantly, she would use it to find Rosalynde.

Seren herself had never witnessed its use, but they knew it was precious and powerful, and in its current state, their mother could easily use it to ferret them out.

Gently, Seren lifted up the scrying stone. The instant she touched it, the interior began to shift, the stone swirling and billowing through the marbled depths like a storm made of crystal. Helpless to do aught but watch, their eyes became affixed to the images forming...

Passed down through the ages, the scrying stone was powerful, indeed. As the story went, even as the Witch Goddess Cerridwen had been sucked into the depths of her watery prison, her screams had formed bubbles that drifted to the surface. The instant her breath returned to the *aether*, it solidified into crystals, the largest being the crystal Seren held in her hands— Merlin's Jewel. In the stone's opaque, vaguely shimmering depths, she saw lithe figures arising from mist... a man ... kneeling... and... Rosalynde, seated on a stump in her nun's habit. Her *glamour* was gone, and she was watching some man kindle his fire.

Arwyn gasped, sounding dismayed. "She has revealed herself," she said.

Seren tilted her head to continue watching. "Not necessarily... the crystal would naturally reveal her to us; it would never be fooled by her *glamour*."

"What should we do?"

The sun was rising, sending tendrils of soft pink in through their windows. Soon the palace would wake, with a great swell of breath, like a stone beast arising from slumber.

And soon... Morwen was bound to return.

Some part of Seren longed to ask the crystal where she might be, but both she and her sister were still beguiled by the images the crystal had revealed to them —Rosalynde... in the company of... was he her champion?

And then Seren looked closer... recognizing the man. "Sweet, merciful Goddess!"

"What is it, Seren?"

Seren's hand flew to her lips in wonder. "That, my dearest Arwyn, is Giles de Vere."

Arwyn's entire face screwed with confusion. "*Your* betrothed?"

"So it seems."

The sisters lifted their gazes to peer into one another's eyes, blinking in surprise. Why would Seren's betrothed be Rosalynde's champion? Could it be that he was acting in her mother's behalf? What were they doing together?

"Will she be alright?"

Seren's brows drew together and she shook her head, but she said, "He did not strike me as an evil man, but who can say, Arwyn. The Goddess works in mysterious ways."

"What should we do?"

"I don't know."

"Should we warn Rose?"

Seren inhaled a fortifying breath, though she still could not wrest her gaze away from the crystal. "Nay," she said. "We daren't risk it... not now. Instead, we must pray he was sent to aid her."

The sounds of people stirring resounded from the hall, doors opening, whispers filtering in under the crack beneath their door. "If we mean to, we must go now," urged Arwyn, peering nervously at the door.

At last, Seren lifted her gaze from the crystal. "What about the scrying stone?"

"We cannot leave it."

But it was too big to carry afoot. Morwen had a special leather pouch that hung over her pommel, but they would have no horse to carry it, and even now, it felt inordinately heavy in Seren's hands, because within its hallowed depths, it bore all the possibilities of the *aether*—all things to come, all things past, and all things that lingered in twilight.

For a long, long moment, the sisters stared at one another, their gazes shifting back and forth, one to another, and each to Merlin's Jewel, where Rosalynde and her dubious champion remained visible.

Giles de Vere had abandoned the woodpile, and moved to sit beside their sister, and Arwyn said softly, "Do it, Seren. The Goddess will forgive you."

Ancient and irreplaceable, there was no other scrying stone of its worth in the entire World. There were certainly others with less power, but this was the only crystal born of the breath of the dragon. Like the Book of Secrets, it was priceless. "Do it," Arwyn said, urging her.

Seren, gave her sister a nod of accord, and with one last glance at the door—lest Morwen enter and surprise them—and an inhale of breath for courage, she lifted her arms high and brought them crashing down, releasing the ancient stone to the floor. It shattered at their feet, exploding into a thousand shards, its vague sea-green glow at once diminished, like a flame extinguished.

At once, both girls bent to grab a small piece—if only for posterity—and then, shoving the pieces of Merlin's Jewel into their rucksacks, they left what remained on the floor, rushing to the door.

16

I t was only as she inhaled her supper that Rosalynde realized how very famished she was and how long she'd gone without supping—not since yesterday morn, long hours before leaving London. Goddess forgive her, but never had she enjoyed the consumption of cooked flesh with such abandon. She had relished every small bite, including the charred skin. Consequently, as her mouth was moving without any true purpose of speaking, she learned a number of things.

First, the power of mind over body was fascinating. She had been too preoccupied to allow herself to feel any hunger, and now that she had essentially acknowledged it, she was like a wild beast, snarling over her food, and eating with all the eagerness of a London beggar.

Secondly, Wilhelm of Warkworth was conflicted. She recognized his love and his concern, even as she acknowledged his anger. It was there in his eyes and his voice when he spoke to his lord brother. Whether it was because of Lady Ayleth, or some other grievance, she hadn't any clue, but it wasn't really her concern.

Thirdly, the man didn't seem know what to do with her, though he was perfectly content to ignore her. Unlike his brother—who couldn't seem to keep his eyes off her—every once in a while, he peered out of the corner of one eye and then swiftly away when she met his gaze.

And fourthly, like a child looking for validation, Wilhelm talked a *lot*, rambling on and on about everything, from the difficulty of catching cony, to the idiosyncrasies of a good war horse, to the dissembling of Stephen. Rose wondered if Giles realized that a simple thank you from him might actually tame his brother's prattling. And nevertheless, since it wasn't forthcoming, Wilhelm carried on. And on. And on...

Now, he took it upon himself to name every known infraction Stephen ever made—everything from the breaking of his oaths to her father, to the handling of the kingswoods.

But, of course, neither of these men had any inkling they were speaking about Rosalynde's father, and she hadn't any inclination to tell them. She sat quietly, watching, listening.

"You were not there, Giles. I distinctly heard him say—with his own mouth—he would overturn Henry's forest laws," Wilhelm talked through greasy fingers, as he gnawed at his bone, spitting out slivers. "Still he has not. Twelve years of lies and more lies."

The differences between these two brothers couldn't be more distinctly evident by the manner of their supping. Wilhelm, dark and brooding, tore after his meal with more zeal than Rosalynde had, much to her chagrin because it wasn't very attractive to watch. But at least she had the veil to hide her greasy teeth and lips. Giles, on the other hand, purposely sliced his meat from the bone, placing the neat slices into a growing pile. "I have no issue with the kingswoods," Giles said. "As it stands, there's hardly any boar left anywhere. At least Henry's Forest Law protects them."

Wilhelm argued, "There's boar in Pickering and Inglewood."

"For now, and yet the instant he overturns that charter, every man and his brother will hunt them. They'll be gone before you know it."

Wilhelm harrumphed. "And you think that man honors Henry's Law because he cares about boar? Nay, brother. He maintains those kingswoods because he covets them for himself."

Giles offered his brother a lift of his brow. "There's much I do not respect about our king, but I warrant he hasn't time for hunting, Will. Gossip doesn't behoove you."

Wilhelm growled, tossing away his bone, sliding Rosalynde a prickled glance. Meanwhile, Giles leaned back against the stump Rose had been seated upon earlier, staring contemplatively into the fire, and every now and again he looked at Rose, studying her as though she were a suspicious roll of knucklebones.

Only now that she had a bit of food in her belly and she could think more clearly, she realized that, whilst she continued wearing the veil, the worst case might be that her eye color would change, and Giles might note it. Else-wise, much of her face remained hidden, and if either of these men suspected something, there was hardly any chance they would rip the veil from her face to reveal her.

And nevertheless, she could not abide the smell of the veil now that she had cony grease all over it, and if the itchy fabric wasn't annoying enough, the foul odor made her long to rip it off and toss it away.

Truly, now that she was away from London, there

was no reason to keep the *glamour* or the veil, save that these two arguing brothers had already seen her face, and how would she explain it? She had but needed the *glamour* to escape London without being recognized. Here on the road, it was enough to be wearing the habit.

She tried her best to ignore Giles, eating quietly, listening intently, and therein also discovered precisely where they were—not in any of the kingswoods, so it seemed, even despite their heated discussion over the subject.

Long past Darkwood, Giles had directed them to some small woodlot south of Whittlewood and Salcey, where only small quarry survived, which was indubitably the reason the woods seemed so quiet. Sadly, it couldn't even be called a forest. Unlike Darkwood, with its thick cluster of trees, the woods were thin and sparse. There was hardly any place for hart or boar to roam or hide—nor for that matter, any place for *anyone* to hide, which, in essence, was the deciding factor in Rosalynde's decision to leave—the sooner the better.

So much as she appreciated these brothers grim and their sweet, lovely horses—and so much as she'd like to believe the Goddess had sent them to aid her— she had no choice.

Rhiannon once told her that following the will of the Goddess should be easy. It was only difficult if you were attempting to force your own will over the will of the Mother. So, if, at some point, all of life seemed to be conspiring, it was time to reexamine one's decisions.

Therefore, so much as she had hoped Giles could be her very own champion, it mustn't be so. It was too difficult to be in his company; and there were many,

many reasons to leave, only a few to stay. And truly, considering that she hadn't actually anticipated finding herself a champion at all, there was only one true reason to stay: the mare.

On the other hand, when she considered all the many reasons to flee, they were a multitude.

Most significantly, there was the matter of the warding spell—without it, she would never sleep at night. And, when it came right down to it, two surly brothers with shiny swords were hardly any defense against her mother, and, anyway, both men were far too immersed in their own squabbles to have any sense for impending danger.

Moreover, even if Rosalynde could manage to find a good warding spell to be used without a proper pentacle, she was afraid they would be shocked to see her cast it, despite that they could no longer witness the effects it wrought upon the *aether*—startlingly beautiful formations, not unlike fae dust, or tiny, winking stars.

Sadly, most folks could no longer see the things a *dewine* saw, nor hear the voice of the Goddess. But to a *dewine's* eyes, *all* things were made of stars—even this... strange appeal betwixt her and Giles. Rose felt it like an annoying tug at her heart and a crackle in the air, and it was hardly as comforting as she'd imagined it should be. It filled her with incredible angst, and she had more than enough of that already with worries over Morwen.

So, then, whilst Wilhelm continued to complain about Stephen's reluctance to overturn her father's Forest Law, despite his promise to do so, Rosalynde planned her escape...

If she could manage to slip into those puny woods, perhaps these contenders would be too busy thinking up ways to best each other and too replete to bother coming after her—at least for a while. As exhausted as she was—and, sweet Goddess she was—she knew they must be all the more so, because at least she had managed to sleep last night and a little while in the saddle.

And anyway, neither of these brothers should care about a silly nun. Quite to the contrary, they should be pleased to be rid of her—and, no matter, Rosalynde didn't believe they should trouble themselves with a search when they had days and days left to travel on their own account. Warkworth, she'd learned, lay far, far to the north—nearly as far as Aldergh. It was a week yet to Neasham, or so Giles had said, but that was by horse, and she would be afoot. Neasham was south of Aldergh—perhaps only halfway—and yet, so much as Rosalynde loathed to add another week or more to her travels, if she managed to hide herself well enough, even from these contentious brothers, she'd arrive at Neasham, long, long after they'd departed. Then, she could entreat upon the sisters to sell her a horse—and so what if they should happen to mention a silly nun from their travels. She would have more than enough of the *philter* remaining to cast one final *glamour*—one that would mask her dress as well as her face. They would see her as a luckless traveler and she would tell them that she had been robbed. If they wondered why she still had money to purchase a horse after being burgled, she would explain that she'd hidden the gold marks in the hem of her gown —and in fact, she could show them, and once she was gone, that would be the last of her lies.

As for the dream about Rhiannon... perhaps, after all, she wasn't alone. Perhaps Rhi would guide her, and she must trust her sister above all.

"You've been gone a long time, Giles. Not everything is as it was. And nevertheless, I'd not steer you wrongly."

Wilhelm's tone was resentful, and yet, Giles didn't answer, despite that Rosalynde sensed there was a pointed message in his brother's statement. Perhaps he'd fallen asleep? If she hadn't so much on her mind, Wilhelm's rambling would have had the same numbing effect on her.

At last, she decided that the time had arrived —*now* before she lost her nerve.

If she hurried, she could still find a good place to conceal herself before the sun set.

Scooping up her Book, she got up, belly roiling, though not over the meal she'd so ravenously consumed.

Without a word, she took the *grimoire* and bounded away, abandoning the cloak. She didn't want them to suspect, and she didn't need the cloak anyway. She'd only taken it because Arwyn had given it to her and it would be easy enough to cast another warming spell once she was safely away.

17

Alas, nothing ever happened quite as one expected. It was Wilhelm, not Giles, who sprang to his feet to follow. "Sister!" he called out, and Rosalynde winced, pretending not to hear him. He shouted a little louder, and she feared he might wake his brother. "Sister, wait!"

Goddess please!

Was she never going to be away?

Realizing that she couldn't possibly outrun the man, she halted, turning to face the lout, pasting a serene smile on her face, and raising the Book to hide her quickened breath. "What may I do for you, Wilhelm?"

Cheeks flushing, the big man cast a nervous glance toward their camp, where his brother remained seated by the fire, still sleeping, judging by his repose.

"I beg pardon if I have offended," he said, and Rose softened at the pleading quality of his voice.

"How can I help you?"

"I should like to confess my sins," he said, his face twisting with what appeared to be regret—or perhaps it was only indigestion. Rosalynde couldn't tell. She had a grumble in her belly herself.

"My lord, I am no priest," she protested.

He smiled awkwardly. "And I am no lord—base-born," he said sheepishly, and then he stood, scratching his head, then gesturing to her book. "In truth, I wouldst simply pray... if you might. 'Tis been an age since I have done so, and I am not certain God will listen."

"God always listens," she reassured him.

Smiling gratefully, he nevertheless glanced back toward their camp, then swept out a hand, gesturing nervously. "Shall we walk apart?"

With a sigh, Rosalynde peered back at Giles, feeling her opportunity slipping away. Even now, the sun was lowering.

"Please, Sister," he begged, and put a hand beneath her elbow to lead her away from Giles, deeper into the woods. "You see... I fear I've dishonored my father by dishonoring my brother..."

Rosalynde felt like a lamb being led to her slaughter and she sorely hoped his God would be listening, because she hadn't any notion how to help this man. She was very glad her grimace remained hidden behind her veil. Her sister Elspeth had been far more dutiful at her prayers. More than not, Rosalynde had spent her days at the priory dreaming of new adventures, and if, in truth, she knew the hours of prayer, it was only so she could better plan when she could escape into the woods to forage. "Alas, I love a lady my brother was promised to..."

Rosalynde's brow furrowed, curiosity getting the best of her. "Lady Ayleth?" she asked, and that same prickle of envy reared unexpectedly.

Wilhelm lifted a bushy black brow. "Perchance you knew her?"

Rose shook her head. "Nay, I but guessed. I heard

you speaking of the lady on the road and I wondered who she was. So she and Giles must have been betrothed?"

"Never," he said. "Though I am quite certain it disappointed her uncle when my brother left for the seminary." He looked even more discomforted, scratching his head, leading her farther afield. "You see, what ails me is that Ayleth loved my brother, and even now that she's gone, I envy him her love—particularly so, because it seems to me that Giles never cared."

Rosalynde flicked a finger across the vellum, feeling oddly defensive over Giles and his honor.

"Wilhelm, envy is a sin, love is not," she explained, telling him what she thought the Goddess might want him to know. "But you cannot fault yourself for loving Lady Ayleth. In truth, you cannot force a heart to love where it should any more than you may force it to love where it should not. And, besides, my Lord Giles *must* have cared for the lady; did he not say he would give alms for her soul?"

In answer, Wilhelm peered into the treetops, mayhap supplicating for strength. "Aye, and, truly, it does soothe my soul to know he offers alms, though... I confess... it was all I could do not to weep blood tears when King Stephen offered my brother an earldom and Lady Seren Pendragon to wed."

Her attention well and duly caught by the mention of her sister, Rosalynde turned to face him.

Wilhelm's eyes were narrowed. She could see the fury burning in them. "The lady comes to him with a generous emolument, and Stephen himself would presume to pay for the wedding. And yet, 'tis not so much that I begrudge him a bride—nor even a title, Sister, 'tis..."

"I notice Lady Seren does not travel with you," she interrupted, wanting desperately to know more about her sister and Giles. "Did your brother not accept?"

Wilhelm looked annoyed by the change in subject. "Of course, he did, only on the condition that he return six months hence to take his vows—like some poppet."

"I see," said Rose, wishing vehemently that luck would have found her traveling with her sister—except that it would have meant leaving Arwyn alone, and some part of her was grateful they were still together.

And more, she didn't wish to think of Giles and Seren together, though why that should be true, she didn't care to explore.

And still, too bad for Seren, because Rosalynde had already determined Giles was an honorable man. Her sister would be so fortunate. Torn between sisterly pride and some burgeoning sense of envy, she longed to ask Wilhelm what his brother thought of her beautiful sister, but that was all the more reason for Rosalynde to leave—now, before Giles de Vere had the chance to undermine her good sense and will. The last thing she intended was for any man to come betwixt her and her sweet sister—as a woman must surely have come between these brothers. "Do you not love your brother?" she asked gently, laying a hand on his arm.

"I do," said Wilhelm. "I would give my life for Giles."

His brotherly admission made Rosalynde both happy and sad. She, too, would die to save her sisters, and this doubtless was the reason she had insisted upon taking the *grimoire* to Elspeth. Not only did she believe she was the most capable, but she had known in her heart that neither gentle Seren nor innocent Arwyn could ever manage such a harrowing quest.

"How did Lady Ayleth die, if you would pardon my asking?"

The warrior's countenance darkened. "Burned alive," he said, and his face was a sudden mask of fury. "By the Count of Mortain and his Welsh witch."

Morwen. Sweet fates, how many more atrocities had her mother wrought in this world? Her evil was like a poison filtering through the veins of this land, destroying all it touched.

"They came in the wee hours with torches. I lost two sisters, as well as an elder brother, and my—our sire."

"And Lady Ayleth?"

Rosalynde's heart wrenched for the man.

Wilhelm nodded glumly, and the grief-stricken look on his face tugged at her heart. It was no wonder he was so tormented. "I should have died that night with my kinsmen," he explained. "Alas, I was away with a message to Arundel. Imagine my shock to return and encounter my home in ruins."

Poor man.

She closed her arm around his. "Wilhelm," she entreated, "do you love your brother truly?"

"I do," he vowed. "More than aught I wish to purge my heart. I suffer night terrors, Sister Rosalynde. I cannot wrest these images from my mind, neither waking, nor sleeping."

"Oh, Wilhelm..." Rosalynde shook her head with compassion. "I... I am ... so... so sorry." Hot tears brimmed in her eyes, and she swallowed, with some difficulty. "Do not worry, my brother. God will forgive you." She sensed this was precisely what he needed to hear. "I feel the love in your heart is greater than your ire, else you would never have sought my counsel."

Wilhelm nodded fervently. "Still, I worry," he persisted, his eyes dark with torment. "So much as envy is my burden, I'd not lose my brother, good Sister. I fear it more than I fear my own death. Giles is all that remains of my blood kin, and he is too arrogant and too certain of himself, despite that his blade has never shed a drop of blood. He is an innocent, learned by books and the Church, not by his blade, and in this day and age, I fear for his safety, even as I fear for my soul."

Rosalynde's brows lifted. "Art certain of that?" she asked, because she did not feel it could be true. She did not read auras so well as Elspeth, but Giles was no innocent. And, to be sure, neither did he strike her as an arrogant man, nor a man who took his responsibilities lightly. It was only now, as she stood conversing with Wilhelm that she suspected it might have been folly to try to escape him. She had a good sense that his honor would not allow him to leave her to the mercy of the world at large. And now that she understood... she realized that he had been far more patient with his wayward brother than even was prescribed. If either of them had hubris to be disposed of, it was Wilhelm, not Giles. Giles had treated Wilhelm with enduring patience, even as the elder man had baited him, and now she understood that Wilhelm thought his age and experience to be worthier than his brother's. She was not fit to make such a judgement, but she knew in her heart that it took a great man to wield unyielding patience over anger, and a strong mind to understand that his brother's temperament was not a sign of disloyalty, but rather, a tormented and confused mind.

"Only tell me what to do," Wilhelm pleaded.

Rosalynde lifted her hand, laying it upon his whiskered cheek, advising him from her heart. "Go to your brother, Will. Tell him all you have told me. Pledge him your obeisance, as it should be... as your father no doubt would have wished."

He shook his head adamantly, lifting a hand and pushing Rosalynde's away. "Nay, you do not understand... I cannot turn my face and allow my brother to endanger himself, when I am the one who knows better. He is my lord, but he is my brother, and I would prostrate myself if I could, but for the sake of his life and for the sake of Warkworth, I will not!"

Rosalynde didn't have any opportunity to disabuse him of his notions. Just then, a darkling shadow passed over their heads, like a bird of prey... circling...

She realized only belatedly that they were standing in an open glade, ripe for the plucking. Her first thought was for Morwen's ravens, but all at once, the woodlands grew cold and dark, and she longed for her mother's cloak—that profane coat she could scarce bear to touch, much less wear, no matter how chilled she might be.

The shadow captured Wilhelm's attention as well, and he glanced up, his face contorting, and even as his chin tipped skyward, Rosalynde heard the sound of Rhiannon's voice—so terrifying in its incarnation that it wasn't possible to feel relieved. For eight long months she had longed to know if her sister lived, and if Rhi had broken her silence, it was only because there was danger.

Run! she screamed.

Only Rosalynde heard the warning, and for the briefest instant, she wasn't certain that what she'd heard was real. Her instant of doubt was her undoing.

She peered into the boughs and saw it—enormous and terrifying!

Run! Rhiannon shouted again. *Run, Rose, run!*

This time, Rosalynde bolted, but Wilhelm—a giant bulwark of a man, perhaps thinking himself invincible—stood fast, unsheathing his sword. The blade left its scabbard as the shadow—large as a flying horse—swooped into the glade, diving toward Rose.

She tripped as Wilhelm stepped into the Shadow's path, but he didn't have any chance to raise the sword. He cried out in pain and surprise as the weapon flew from his hand.

Rosalynde screamed.

18

R *un, Rose, run!*
What happened next happened so swiftly Rosalynde could scarce anticipate it. There was no place to hide. Nowhere to run. No time to think. Her immediate concern for the *grimoire,* she seized the book and scrambled to her feet, searching desperately for somewhere to hide, only to realize with a sinking heart that she couldn't leave Wilhelm.

Her heart pounding fearfully, she turned to find the Shadow Beast had pinned him to the ground, its black wings pummeling. The creature cast back an enormous deformed head, opening its bloody beak, to give a terrifying shriek, and then returned to pecking at Wilhelm's head, as he thrashed the air before him. Inexplicably, though the beast drew blood, Wilhelm's fists could not find purchase, and in the end, he screamed piteously, lifting both hands to defend his face.

Rosalynde swallowed her fear.

Sweet, sweet Goddess. She had never witnessed anything of this sort—nor even dreamt about it in her night terrors. Neither did she remember any such beast from the drawings in the Book of Secrets—its ebony form pulsing, the edges of its body indistinct and billowy, like smoke. It was impossible to say what shape it held, because, like a murder of crows soaring altogether, its form swelled and ebbed, changing and reforming—first in the shape of a monstrous raven, then a man, then a serpent, curling around Wilhelm's body and choking his breath, so he could no longer scream.

Rosalynde stood frozen, uncertain what to do. But she couldn't do nothing, and she couldn't leave an innocent man to die only because he'd tried to protect her.

Water.

Desperate to help, she held out a trembling palm. Never taking her eyes off the twisting beast, she filled her palm with water, and, dropping the *grimoire*, she closed her other hand about her palm, forming a small lump of ice. She hurled it, hoping if naught else to get the beast's attention, but to Rosalynde's horror, it passed through the Shadow Beast, smacking Wilhelm on the temple and the thrashing warrior went frighteningly still.

So did the beast.

Its head spun unnaturally, its giant beady eyes fixing on Rosalynde. Slowly, deliberately, it released its prey, uncoiling itself from around Wilhelm's body, and with another ungodly screech, it flew at Rose.

Rose screamed, and to her horror, it was only belatedly that she remembered it wasn't her the monster wanted. It was the *grimoire*, and rather than pursue her when she had already abandoned the Book, it fell upon the sacred volume, eddying about the Book of Secrets, like a tempest, lifting the tome from the ground with a long-speared tail.

Finding her courage where only seconds ago she'd

been as shivery as the Beast itself, she turned, and dove after the book—the only solid form in the midst of the shadow. Locking her arms about the book, she held on for dear life.

She was vaguely aware that Wilhelm revived. With a ferocious growl, he reclaimed his sword, pouncing after them, the look on his face as fierce as a bear. Shouting obscenities, he swung wildly at the Shadow, narrowly missing Rosalynde's shoulder, as the gleaming blade slid through the creature without purchase.

It was going to take her *grimoire*! There was naught she could do to stop it. Sweet fates—Mother Goddess!

Trying to shake her free, the beast whipped Rosalynde about like a sheet in the wind, howling as it raged, lifting both Rosalynde and the *grimoire* skyward, with scarcely any effort. It was only then she spied the necklace it wore, dangling like a carrot—a shining bauble bound to a chain, with a glowing crystal. Fear urged her not to release the *grimoire*, but something else, a voice ageless as time, compelled her else-wise.

Let go, Rose. Seize the reliquary.

Nay. If she did so, she would lose the book forever —if she released it, the beast would fly away. She would fail. She would fail. The book would be gone. Morwen would win.

No, no, no, no...

Wilhelm continued to swing his sword, snarling furiously as the sword missed time and again. Tiring of his efforts, the Beast's viper-like tail cut through the air, catching Wilhelm beneath the knees and spilling him again to the bracken.

Sweet, sweet fates. Rosalynde felt the book slipping

now, and she curled her fingers more tightly around the vellum, whispering rites to hold it fast.

Let go.

Nay, she thought... *nay... nay...* but so often intuition was a gift from the Goddess—a gift too many failed to heed.

Let go.

Now.

Crying out, Rosalynde dragged herself up and swung closer to the bauble, dropping the book as her fingers caught the cold metal.

Bind it, Rose.

The reliquary and chain cut into her palm, searing her flesh as the Shadow Beast squealed in triumph, catching the *grimoire* with its mutating tail, curling around the book.

Now, bind the Beast.

Rosalynde didn't know binding words—and nevertheless, even as she lamented the fact, strange words sprang to her lips.

> I call the fifth to me!
> Goddess hear my plea!
> Of smoke and mist you might be born.
> Here I bind you now in mortal form.

Right before her eyes, the Shadow Beast began to coalesce into a more solid form—into the shape of a man, still with enormous black wings. Once more, Wilhelm rushed forward to pierce the creature with his sword, but he ventured no closer than the breadth of the creature's wings. Its leathery appendages smacked him away, as easily as though he were no more than a flea.

Landing more than twenty feet away, his look dazed, Wilhelm sat, staring in horror as the creature put talons into Rosalynde's waist, clutching her so brutally that she thought it must have broken her flesh. She cried out in pain and terror, and it was then Giles appeared, tearing through the woods atop his black courser, and what he did next took Rosalynde's breath away...

As her spell solidified the beast, Giles charged them, his every move as darkly sinuous as that of the Shadow Beast's, his movements as choreographed as a macabre dance—a dance of death. To her desperate eyes, it happened as though in slow motion. Once he cleared the boughs of low-lying trees, he rose up on the back of his courser, unsheathing a shimmering golden blade and wielding it so expertly it appeared to be an extension of his being—and he, an extension of the horse.

That sword—it glowed unlike anything Rosalynde had ever seen before. Her eyes transfixed on the haloed metal, even as the creature cut its talons deeper into her flesh.

She shouted the binding words again...

> I call the fifth to me!
> Goddess hear my plea!
> Of smoke and mist you might be born.
> Here I bind you now in mortal form.

Crying out, the creature thrust its black talons even deeper into her middle, and Rosalynde's eyes teared with pain. But, then, just as the Beast hoisted her up, dropping her, only to catch her again more securely, preparing to fly away, Giles leapt off his mare, spinning through the air like a whirling blade. His shining sword caught the beast at its neck, severing the head.

The Shadow Beast opened its claws, releasing Rosalynde and plummeted to the ground. She fell with a thud and a yelp of pain, and barely had time to roll out of the way before the creature came tumbling into the bracken.

Stunned, Wilhelm remained seated on his bottom, staring with his mouth open.

Rosalynde righted her dress, crawling over to seize the *grimoire*, and rose to her feet as Giles knelt beside the creature with his bloodstained sword still in his hand.

With trembling limbs, she ventured over to join him. But when she looked down into the Shadow Beast's face, she gasped in horror. "It's Mordecai!"

"What is a Mordecai?"

Rosalynde shook her head, her face pale as parchment. "Not what, but whom... he's—"

Before their eyes, the creature writhed one final time, losing its wings and mutating into the shape of a man. His youth fell away, withering his flesh until it turned to dust, and without so much as a breeze, the dust rushed into the reliquary still tangled in Rosalynde's hand—vanishing... as though it had been sucked into the reliquary. Swallowing convulsively, she peered at the bauble in her hand... and the cuts and burn in her palm, then tossed the reliquary away, thinking at once of her sisters...

She'd had no idea such things were possible, and now, she feared she'd left Arwyn and Seren to their doom. "No," she whispered.

"Where the hell did you learn to do that?" demanded Wilhelm, his face bloodied and scarred.

Giles turned to look at his brother, who was still

seated on his rump. "In the seminary," he said evenly, and Rose screwed her face, casting a questioning look at Wilhelm, wondering how that could possibly be true.

At this point, her wimple and veil were gone—her *glamour* as well, judging by the way Wilhelm was looking at her—as though she had suddenly sprouted another head.

"You knew him?" Giles asked, dismissing his brother, and turning to question Rosalynde, with one brow arched and his pupils darker than they had ever appeared before. They penetrated her to her very soul, probing her secrets and promising to reveal them.

Alas, it was past time to confess.

Come what may, she could not keep that *grimoire* from her mother without help—and clearly, this man had what it took to keep her safe. There was no doubt in her mind now: He was sent by the Goddess.

"Aye," Rosalynde said, clutching her side, grimacing with pain. "I knew him."

"And?"

She winced, more over the pain of her confession than over the pain in her middle. "Alas, I have a confession to make," she said, looking Giles's straight in the face. "I am neither a nun, nor am I in route to Neasham."

He tilted her a knowing glance, his black eyes shining, his gaze betraying little surprise. "And is that all?"

She might as well confess *everything*. "Nay.... I was the one who stole your horse..."

Both his brows lifted now, and still he pressed her, "Something more?"

Rosalynde shook her head sheepishly, realizing

the words must be said. "My mother's name is Morwen," she said, tears forming in her eyes, and she then
buckled to her knees, the edges of her vision black-
ening as pain shot through her side.

19

In a motion equally as fluid as his effort on his horse, Giles re-sheathed his sword and swept Rosalynde into his arms, leaving Wilhelm and the horse to follow. "You're injured," he said, in a far gentler tone than she'd expected. And yet, even as Rosalynde clung to her Book, she was terrified.

That was Mordecai—her mother's disciple—but what in the name of the Goddess was he? *A gargoyle?*

Her brain still could not reconcile what she'd witnessed.

Wilhelm recovered himself far more quickly than she did, hurrying ahead, snatching a blanket from the back of his horse and shaking it out as Giles carried Rosalynde over and placed her gently atop it. He laid her down with such care that it made her throat tight.

She peered up, clutching his tunic. "Thank you," she said, groaning in pain as he released her.

"I beg pardon, but..." His gaze fell to her waist, where her gown was soaked with her own blood, and Rosalynde blinked, glancing up again, meeting his gaze. "I would see what damage was done."

"It doesn't hurt," she lied, and tried to push him away. Even now, she didn't wish to explain. If he would just leave her be and go away, she would heal herself and be done. Already, the blood flow was ebbing. If he hadn't already determined who Morwen was, she was beginning to doubt the wisdom in revealing herself.

He caught her by the wrist and said, "I would see it with my own eyes... with your permission and your pardon."

Realizing he wouldn't let it go, Rosalynde nodded dumbly, and let him push her gently back onto the blanket. He produced a knife from his boot and sliced the gown at her midriff, so he could see her wound, but still salvage some semblance of modesty.

"There's a lot of blood," he told her, his face crestfallen, and Rosalynde peered into his dark eyes, her own eyes filling with telltale tears as she lifted her hand instinctively to heal herself. Not understanding her intent—perhaps thinking her too modest, he once again caught her hand, holding it firmly in his own. "I don't know how deep it is," he said. "You shouldn't disturb it."

Rosalynde was afraid... though not about the wound. For the first time in her life, someone besides her sisters was looking at her... perhaps not with love, but concern, and it begged her to speak her truth. She lay exposed—literally—and trust was the only means to her salvation.

Inhaling a fortifying breath, she shook free of his hand, holding his gaze, and pleading with her eyes for him to allow her to do what she must.

Giles frowned but didn't resist, and she peered down to inspect her wound. Now that the shock was wearing off, it was beginning to ache, but not for long. She put a hand over the torn flesh and whispered the necessary words—not out loud. It wasn't necessary, and she would be embarrassed for him to hear her.

Slowly, her flesh began to close before his eyes. *They* couldn't see her *magik* working, but they could witness the end result—healed flesh, only stained by blood as proof of what she had endured. Except the burn on her palm remained. Healed though it might be, the scar remained dark... and she glanced down, moving her dress to find that her puncture marks were black as well.

Alas, there was no sense holding anything back now...

These men, too, had suffered by her mother's hand, and if anything, it gave her hope of convincing them to ally with her. She had no doubt any longer that Giles was her champion—hers, not Seren's. No one could have done what he did, and she would be dead now without his help.

Without being asked, Rosalynde proceeded to explain all that she dared to explain, beginning with the details of her *glamour* spell. It wasn't much different than a lady with *maquillage*, she told them, only this face paint was not powder or cream, it was a mask woven of *aether*, a suggestion by the Goddess to give mortal eyes what she wished them to see.

She went on to explain about the *grimoire*, as well —how important it was to deliver the Book to Elspeth. Alas, Aldergh was the only place she knew to take it. Her sister Rhiannon was being held at Blackwood by agents of her mother's, and she had no hope of infiltrating that stronghold without help—nor could she ultimately be certain the *grimoire* alone would be enough to give Rhiannon the means to overcome her captors. After all, the only place she felt certain would receive her without sending her back to Stephen was Aldergh. Malcom Scott had once been a vassal of the Usurper's, but he was no longer. Stephen had named him an enemy to the crown.

"I know who he is," said Giles.

Of course, he did. There seemed to be very little of her story that surprised him. But, all through the telling, Wilhelm stared at her, his dark eyes wide with horror, his shredded and blood-stained face like the Shadow Beast, contorting with every word she spoke. Only now that she had revealed herself, she was entirely at their mercy and she was too far into her explication to pretend it was aught less than it was. "I am *not* a witch," she explained. "I'm a *dewine*." But, when both men furrowed their brows, she relented. "Very well, I *am* witch. But this is not what you suppose."

She didn't like that word—witch—because of what it meant to others. She was a child of the Earth Mother, a Maiden pledged to the *hud*, but for all these men knew of the Craft of the Wise, witchery was as good as any word she might use. And nevertheless, she endeavored to explain that in their native tongue, they were known as *dewines*, not witches. Translated more precisely, they were enchantresses, but also healers, prophets, seers. As with any art, not everyone had the same skills, and certainly not all were dark.

"And your mother?"

"Whatever Morwen may be, her heart lies far from the principles of our tenets, which dictate we do good, harm none." She looked warily between the brothers, trying to gauge their thoughts, but there was no help for it. Here and now, she would propose treason, and they might as well know it. She held Giles's gaze, ignoring Wilhelm, realizing that Giles now held her future in his hands. She said, pointedly, "*My mother* is an enemy of the realm, so much as Stephen may not realize... so, too, is his son."

To this, Giles merely nodded, and without a word, he stood, unsheathing the golden blade from his scabbard. He laid it down on the blanket beside her, flicking a glance at his brother. "Do you see that sword?" he asked. "Do you know what it is?"

"'Tis a sword," said Wilhelm, confused.

Rosalynde shook her head.

"Look closer," he bade her, and with Wilhelm peeking over her shoulder, she dared to look closer to read the inscription etched in Latin.

"Mea est ultio, et ego retribuam," she said, and even as she read, the golden serpents in the sword's hilt seemed to slither and the words themselves lifted from the blue steel, doubling in size and igniting before her eyes—*magik.*

Vengeance Is Mine, I Shall Repay.

She blinked, recognizing the passage from her days in the priory. *If your enemy be hungry, feed him; if he be thirsty, give him drink; for in so doing you will heap coals upon his head. Never avenge yourselves... but...* She finished the passage aloud, with sudden revelation, "Leave it to the wrath of God," she whispered, and Giles gave her a nod.

His brother sat utterly still, listening, and Giles finished the passage for Rosalynde, lifting a golden brow. "For it is written that, 'Vengeance is mine, I Shall repay, saith the Lord.'"

Rosalynde peered up, into Giles's face—into his dark knowing eyes, alight with something not entirely holy.

He gave her another short nod, realizing she understood, and then a bow. "I am and ever shall be the wrath of God on Earth, a humble servant of the Palatine Guard."

20

Giles was a Paladin—as formidable a commission as the king's Rex Militum, save that he served the Holy Roman Empire, not the English crown. And yet, he wasn't a priest; he was a man, with all a man's faults, and his body trembled at the sight of the woman peering up at him so haplessly, her expression something akin to horror.

But he knew why she was looking at him that way, and he sensed she understood precisely who—and what—he was.

Her own grandmother had been subject to the laws of the Church, and she'd suffered a heretic's death, burned at the stake by the edict of the Empress's first husband. As it was with the Rex Militum, the Palatine Guardsmen were executioners for the realms, and it was their company who'd been assigned to carry out justice for Morgan Pendragon. After all, it was their task to dispatch enemies of the Church, whether they be heretics... or witches. And yet, his post was a bit of a contradiction, because it was the Prophet Merlin—a Pendragon himself—who'd given them their rites of passage. It was a fact that kept them relegated to the shadows—a stain on the sanctity of the Church.

"You're a Huntsman," she said quietly, though it wasn't a question.

Giles shrugged dispassionately, despite there wasn't a single muscle in his entire body that didn't feel tense, and there was naught apathetic about his thoughts.

"That's perhaps one word for it," he said.

Rosalynde blinked again, and he swallowed now as he studied her face—the same face he'd first spied when he'd encountered her sleeping... and it was *that* face he'd envisioned in his dreams. To look upon it now left him breathless. And, not even the fact that she was Morwen Pendragon's daughter had any tempering effect upon his ardor. It was as though, in truth, as he stood gazing down upon this Daughter of Avalon... all meaning to his life became clear. He was meant to be here... this moment... with her, and not even his true mission in England held the same verity. Somehow, he was meant to be Rosalynde Pendragon's champion, and she was meant... *for what?*

What role had she to play in her mother's demise?

He flicked a glance at her book; understanding dawned.

Avoiding Rosalynde's gaze, he bent to pick up his longsword and then re-sheathed it—another legacy of Merlin's. As it must be for all the men in the Palatine Guard, the sword had been chosen specifically for him, but there remained twelve such swords, all forged from blooms of steel, and containing a special consecrated alloy that glowed faintly in the presence of evil.

This girl was *not* evil. The sword's golden halo had vanished the instant he'd dispatched the Shadow

Beast, and not for an instant during their travels had he felt the low thrum of the finely-honed metal at his hip.

As for Morwen Pendragon... she was another matter entirely. Morwen herself was a demon, and the Church had dispatched Giles—not only to reclaim a valuable seat in his father's name, but to pave the way for the Empress's son to take his rightful place on England's throne.

Now, more than before, he understood that the Church must not confirm the Count of Mortain. Stephen must not be allowed to install his son on the throne. Morwen Pendragon must be stopped at all cost, and Eustace was no more than her poppet. If the king managed to hand the realm to his miscreant son, England would be lost.

And yet, so much as the barons had sworn their fealties to the Empress, neither was Matilda destined to be their savior. She was a woman, and so much as a woman could destroy it, no woman could unite England's barons. It must be Duke Henry, and they must continue to weaken the king's hold and strengthen the resolve of the Church.

Giles had but needed his dispensation to give the illusion he was Stephen's loyal man—to keep those bastards off his lands. Even now, there were ships due to arrive at his port with men enough and supplies enough to begin reconstruction—all save for the stone he must procure, and perhaps that dilemma might be solved now by speaking to the very man whose aid Rosalynde was seeking—the lord of Aldergh. The ex-king's man had access to a sizable quarry, and it was for that reason alone he had managed to construct and maintain such a monstrosity as Aldergh. If the earl of Wallingford could hold back a siege for a year, Aldergh could do it for three.

He realized Rosalynde was still staring at him, perhaps waiting for confirmation. "Aye," he said.

His brother, as always, was clueless. "What is she talking about, Giles?"

He turned to Wilhelm now, gauging how much he could say without betraying his oaths, and then said in jest, "I mustn't be so dreadful with a blade, after all." And he gave his brother a lopsided grin.

Wilhelm tilted him a look of confusion, bemused, perhaps as he should be. More than once Giles had tried to tell him that he was not the man he believed, although if the dispatching of the Shadow Beast wasn't proof enough, there wasn't much more he could say—or do. And nevertheless, he could say this much: "I am sworn to protect the Holy Church from its enemies, no matter what form they take."

Wilhelm pointed into the woods. "What was that?"

Giles shrugged, again. "That... I don't know, brother, but this lady might enlighten us..." He returned his gaze to Rosalynde Pendragon, entreating her with a tilt of his head. "As you were saying, Lady Rosalynde... what, pray tell, is a Mordecai?"

Rosy cheeked, Rosalynde averted her gaze. "He's my mother's... manservant, but... I did not know..." She shook her head, and if she meant to say anything more, her words seemed disinclined to come.

Unwittingly, Giles's attention fell upon the rip in her dress, exposing her middle to his brother's eyes— and for the first time in his life he understood Wilhelm's jealousy over Lady Ayleth. He didn't wish for any man to see Rosalynde this way—not even his staid and loyal brother.

Swallowing hard, Giles walked away, returning a

moment later with the cloak Rosalynde had placed in
his satchel. He tossed it down beside her, and she
pushed it away. "That is my mother's," she said. "I
would not wear it lest I were dying!" And with a bit
more ardor, she added, "'Tis *catskin!*"

Dear God. Cat fur.

Giles grimaced in disgust.

God's truth, the more he knew of the dispossessed
lady of Blackwood, the more thoroughly he disliked
her.

Removing his own cloak, he handed it down to
Rosalynde, pleading wordlessly for her to cover herself, and wondering what was wrong with him that he
had not offered his own cloak long before now. Was he
so poor in spirit that he would only respond to a lovely
face?

Thoroughly displeased with himself as much as
he was with the entire situation, he turned away, com-
manding Wilhelm to disband their camp. "We'll be
leaving at once," he said. And then he sighed. "This
time, we'll keep to the woodlands, out of sight of those
bloody birds."

Wilhelm nodded, and, for once, without any com-
plaint, he rushed to do Giles's bidding.

In the meantime, Giles returned to Rosalynde,
reaching out his hand. "Would you trust me with your
book, Rosalynde? I will keep it safe." And he would.
Now that he understood who and what she was, he
suspected he understood why she had safeguarded
the tome so jealously. "I will put it in my satchel and
guard it with my life."

THE BOOK he was requesting was lying beside her. For all
that he was still in possession of that weapon, he might

simply have taken it, simply by bending to retrieve it. After the feats Rosalynde witnessed in that glade, she would never have challenged him... But... he was asking. *Nicely*. And more... there seemed to be a new accord between them... a thread of familiarity... perhaps only natural after having endured such a harrowing experience.

Nodding, she reached over and lifted up the *grimoire*, handing it over to him, even as her own actions confused her.

How willingly she was now proffering the one thing she'd vowed to die for.

With a nod, Giles took the book, then offered Rosalynde a hand. Alas, if she expected nothing more to come after their previous ordeal, she would have been wrong. A sudden jolt passed from his fingers as their fingers met, and yet, startled though she was, she did not pull away. Once the initial shock passed, it left her with an infusion of warmth that traveled from the tips of her fingers, to the very center of her being, right down to the tips of her toes. She curled them reflexively, because the sensation was so... so... evocative.

Bards crooned about love at first sight... of lords and ladies whose hearts burned as one... and *this* must be how they felt.

Somehow, she sensed that he, too, must have felt it... at least so it seemed by his blink of surprise.

Bound by destiny, to destiny bound,
Another to one, and one to another...

Dizzied by the sensation, Rose wavered on her feet, until Giles caught her and steadied her. Tears sprang to her eyes, because the feeling was so intensely powerful. And nevertheless, oblivious to what was transpiring between them, Wilhelm rushed around, dutifully picking up their belongings and putting out their fire.

Only by now there was another fire burning in Rosalynde's heart... simmering to the very depths of her soul... its heat coloring her skin until every part of her flushed.

> Freely choose, or choose to be free.
> As you will it, so mote it be.

Rosalynde blinked. Quite literally, she saw stars bursting before her eyes, and even as the soft, silken voice breezed through her mind, she realized what it was... She'd heard the voice only once before in her life... back in the glade... whilst the Shadow Beast held her in its talons. It was, she realized with awe, the voice of the goddess.

If only she wished to refuse her gift—if Giles wished to—she was free to do so. All she had to do was release his hand... let go, turn away. Confused though he seemed to be as well, he held her hand firmly, and, sweet fates, even knowing that he was betrothed to her sister, Rosalynde entwined her fingers about his, holding him fast, even as she felt a strange thread weave its way through her belly. Terrified to look away now, she peered straight into his dark, soulful eyes, only begging him to confess the things he was hearing and feeling...

The essence of nature seemed to fold and unfold itself, circling around them, like ribbons of fae dust. And still, Rosalynde dared not release his hand...

And... neither did he release hers, though she realized that, though he must surely feel what she felt, he probably couldn't hear what she heard nor see what she saw.

At long last, Rosalynde took a shuddering breath, withdrawing her hand.

"We are ready to ride at your command," announced Wilhelm. And when he received no response, he said, "Giles?"

Giles blinked twice, then shook his head, as though shaking off his stupor, turning to address his brother, looking as confused as Rosalynde felt.

"Aye," he said. "Let's go." And he turned to Rosalynde again, blinking once more.

21

Precisely as Giles had predicted, Neasham proved to be a solid week's journey, and yet, so much as Rosalynde feared another meeting with her mother's disciples, she secretly reveled in every passing moment she spent warmed by Giles's embrace. Unlike that first day they'd traveled together—before her *glamour* spell faded—he held her jealously, and if no one spoke about what happened in the woodlot, everything between them had changed. She felt it in the way he dared to embrace her—every small gesture, like the hand he rested upon her waist, and the fingers he splayed across her belly. *Sweet fates.* Whenever he dared to touch her that way, she felt a stirring down so deep it stole away her breath.

She was not unlike a poppet, responding to every touch. And it was almost as though he pulled at invisible strings, not out there, in the *aether*, but inside her body, and every tug evoked incredible sensations, from her heart to her womb.

And now she understood what the bards meant by *lovesick*. It was a malady in every sense of the word. She felt fevered, achy, and all week long, her mouth remained parched. Her tongue felt too large for her mouth. And no amount of satiating her thirst made any of these symptoms go away. Moreover, her hands perspired, and she had to remember to unclench them every so oft to let them breathe. To her dismay, even despite the cold, she felt hot and bothered, and the feeling put her nerves on edge, until she felt as though she were one immense ball of emotion, unraveling into the *aether*, like yarn into a weaver's loom, spinning impossible dreams... dreams that revealed the two of them as consorts... and more.

And yet, if he made her body come alive, with scarcely his breath on her nape, he seemed completely unaffected.

So much as they'd slept arm in arm on his pallet, he never once offered Rosalynde more than his warmth. Only since that moment in the woods, he'd treated her with the utmost respect, put her on and off his horse with care, bundling her beneath his cloak, and refusing to allow her out of his sight, save for those moments when he must. And even then, he remained close, sword in hand, and Rosalynde daren't complain again, not after coming so close to death.

For his part, Wilhelm seemed confused by their sudden affinity, casting odd glances. But if he thought Rosalynde wanton for clinging so intimately to his lord brother, she couldn't bring herself to care. Giles made her feel safe, even despite the circumstances. And whether it was because of those feats he'd performed in the glade, or merely the solicitous manner in which he cared for her, it didn't matter. It was an unanticipated pleasure to be coddled, and the feel of his arms awakened something she'd never experienced in her life... *desire*... but desire for what?

Closeness? Companionship? Something more?

Confused and uncertain of her own desires, Rosalynde knew only one thing for sure: Only now that Giles was holding her so covetously did she have any sense of how famished she had been for affection. And nay, it wasn't the same as a chaste hug from her sisters. Somehow, Giles's arms felt so right, and if, in fact, it was wrong, she didn't want to know. For the first time in her life, she felt—perhaps not cherished, nor loved; it was too soon for such devotion—but very intimately connected to another human being not her blood.

As similar as it was to the bond she shared with her twin, it was nevertheless as different as night and day. Certainly, she missed Arwyn, though she had never once *longed* to be held by her sister—not like this.

Nor did her sister's nearness make her breath catch.

And even so, for all that she was experiencing this extraordinary awakening, the mood itself turned grim.

For the most part, little was said between the trio. They rode expediently, rested sparingly, and kept to the woodlands, taking care not to attract undue attention or take unnecessary risks.

Without further ado, Giles seemed to appreciate the import of Rosalynde's mission, and he shared her resolve to see the *grimoire* to safety.

For his part, Wilhelm remained quiet and brooding, and Rosalynde had the sense that he, like her, couldn't quite banish the image of the Shadow Beast from his head. So long as she lived, she would never forget that face... the way it had metamorphosed before her eyes... even now, the memory gave her a shiver, and she suspected that such a being was only conceivable through blood *magik*.

Only now, she understood the tales of those days

before the fall of Avalon in a whole new light—of that boy the Witch Goddess pursued, first in the form of a greyhound, then as an otter, then a hawk, and finally, a hen. Even understanding what she did about her *dewine* heritage, she had always considered those tales to be fanciful versions of the truth, meant to be interpreted. But whatever Mordecai had been in that glade, it was not human, and only sacrificial *magik* could have produced such a creature.

Now she wondered: Perhaps in truth, the distant land of her kinsmen was swallowed by the sea... and perhaps the mists of Wales gave ingress to the Nether Realm.

At the moment, there wasn't much she wasn't prepared to believe—after all, Giles himself was a Paladin.

A Paladin.

A Huntsman for the Church.

A slayer of witches.

Oh, yeah, she'd heard of the inquisitions, and she'd understood there was a danger in revealing herself as a *dewine*, but after all, there was naught larger than life about a man with an axe. Executioners need not be huntsmen, and the employment of an entire company of highly trained assassins assigned to ferreting out and exterminating enemies to the Church had seemed... well, farfetched... until now. By the cauldron, how much her perception of the world had changed since leaving Llanthony, where her gravest concern had been to slip past Ersinius's guards, only to win herself a moment to forage in the woods. Only now, with all that had transpired, did she truly comprehend why her sister Elspeth had been so afraid. Rosalynde was afraid now too, and the simple fact that her escorts were so silent and brooding gave her every indication they were as troubled as she was.

Giles adjusted his arms about her, and Rosalynde sighed, burrowing into the safety of his embrace, wondering again about that bonding spell...

But if she doubted the words she'd heard, she must also doubt the council she'd been given in the glade... to bind that beast with words she'd never heard spoken in all her life.

It was as though the Goddess herself provided her the rites to bind the creature into solid form. Only then could Giles have had any chance to slay it. Because no matter how many times Wilhelm had swung his sword, it never once found purchase. And if she needed proof it was not all a dream, she had the reliquary tucked away with the *grimoire* in Giles's satchel. And if not, she but needed to look at Wilhelm, with his ravaged face, because even after seeing what she was capable of, he had refused to allow her to heal him, distrusting her *magik*, if not so much Rosalynde herself. His bloodstains were gone, but his once handsome face now bore the marks of the creature's talons, scars that were healing slowly on their own, but as dark as her own puncture wounds remained, despite her healing *magik*.

Alas, Mordecai was not her mother's only servant, only her most loyal, and, when he did not return, she would go searching for him, and if she came herself... Goddess help them.

"Do you think the creature is dead?" asked Wilhelm, perhaps sensing the dark turn of Rosalynde's thoughts.

Instinctively, Giles pulled her close when she stiffened over the question. "Aye," he said, and his breath was hot against the back of her neck as he whispered, "It's gone, Rose."

"It must be," she said. "But..."

She couldn't finish, even as a caveat, because it seemed too incredible. And still, she worried about the reliquary in Giles's satchel.

Could Mordecai's spirit have retreated into that unholy relic, waiting to be summoned again by her mother?

The feeling it had given her as she'd held it was... indescribable... like darkness and terror bound together. And then, when Wilhelm returned the trinket after she'd thrown it away, she'd had a sudden vision of her kindred—a hundred *dewine* souls—all cowering in the bowels of the earth, whilst outside the earthen bower... lurked an indefinable and present evil. The image made her shudder, and in response, Giles leaned close again, resting his chin on her shoulder. "Don't think of it," he commanded. "I will protect you."

22

Immediately after spending alms for Lady Ayleth's soul, Wilhelm was preparing again to travel. Grateful for the donation, and perhaps feeling aggrieved for all his troubles and fresh scars, the nuns provided him a sack full of victuals and profuse thanks he endured with flushed cheeks.

Giles perhaps would have provided him the alms, but Rosalynde had stepped forward to offer her own —all five gold marks she'd sewn into the hem of her gown. It was the least she could do for the service these brothers were providing, and she had every faith Elspeth would provide for her once Giles delivered her to Aldergh.

When both men had looked at her with a question in their eyes, she'd merely shrugged. "I did tell you I had five gold marks, did I not?"

And yet, clearly, her heartfelt gesture moved Wilhelm, because a twinkle appeared in the warrior's dark eyes. "Thank you... Lady Rosalynde," he said. The title came diffidently to his lips for the first time since meeting her, and the bear of a man stepped forward to offer one more heartfelt embrace. Rosalynde hugged him fiercely, even as she cast a glance at his brother.

THERE WAS no way around it; Wilhelm *must* return to Warkworth to welcome the supply ships. As important as it was to deliver Rosalynde and her *grimoire*, that was Giles's primary objective, and Wilhelm was the only man he trusted.

Rather than procure another mount, he and Rosalynde would travel together. Greedy perhaps, but he wanted her as close to him as possible, even if it slowed their pace.

She glanced at him now, and his heart squeezed.

She was afraid, he sensed. So, too, was Wilhelm. So was Giles, if the truth be known. And yet, it wouldn't serve anyone to confess the truth. He must keep his wits about him... and what was more, he must keep his sanity. If, ever, his faith had failed him, he must find a way to renew it, because God alone could help them now.

Although his past works had more than oft crippled his faith, he saw the madness behind the Guard's methods. Evil could not be vanquished by might alone, nor could it be won by honor and justice. Indeed, God worked in mysterious ways. And yet, he had few illusions. He was but a lone man, and it would take every means available to defeat this rising evil.

So much depended upon his duty to the Guard—and now, to Rosalynde—that his shoulders felt heavy with the burden. But now Wilhelm understood so much without having to be given explanations, and he and his brother had found a new accord. Mounted now, and ready to ride, Wilhelm sought his gaze, and Giles could see the uncertainty nestled in his dark eyes. His elder brother and self-appointed guardian would never willingly abandon his side. "Art certain, Giles?"

Giles nodded. "Now that you... *know*... I trust you most to see to what must be done. Rosalynde and I will continue together." There was great meaning in the words that followed. "I need you, my brother." And one day, when he could, he would reward his loyalty.

His brother's face was pinched, worried, and Giles could tell that he was reluctant to go. But, for all that they'd endured and all the discord that had passed between them, Giles trusted now that he would heed his commands, down to the letter. Their relationship, too, had changed—as thoroughly as with Rosalynde—even despite that they had yet to speak of it.

Later, when they had a moment alone, once the mission was complete, he would explain everything to Wilhelm in far greater detail. And, once the evil in this land was banished, he and Rosalynde—he gazed warmly at the woman standing beside him—would tell stories of this for years to come. Somehow, though he didn't know why he knew it, he knew it to be true. He felt a bond with her that he couldn't explain, nor did he believe for an instant that God had put them together without purpose. And yet... his heart writhed with anguish, because he had a duty to uphold, and so much as he felt in his heart that Rosalynde was destined to be the mother of his babes, he also now understood with a clarity borne of circumstance, how important it was to strengthen his dominion in the north—not merely for the sake of vengeance, but for England.

Wilhelm's knuckles whitened as he gripped his

reins. His eyes said everything his mouth daren't utter. "Have care, my brother," he said.

"Worry not," said Giles. "I am capable."

And to that, the brothers shared the gravest of looks. "Only too well do I know it," said Wilhelm, as he held the courser's reins. "I have been blind, Giles. Fear blinded me to what my eyes should have understood from the moment you returned." And simply so as not to leave words unsaid, his brother offered apologies. "I am sorry," he said.

"Think no more of it," Giles said with a rueful smile.

Wilhelm inclined his head; then, his lips curved ever so slightly. "Mayhap some day you will teach me some of your... tricks?"

Giles lifted his brows. "Tricks?"

Wilhelm's lips turned into a wide, devious grin, and now, more than ever, he looked the part of a mercenary, with a glint in his eyes that matched the glint of his steel, and a set to his shoulders that widened his substantial girth. His scars alone were enough to make a grown man piss himself, if only because to have survived such an ordeal, his strength was unquestionable.

"Godspeed," offered Giles, with a nod.

"WAIT!" Rosalynde said, rushing forward when Wilhelm turned to leave. She had been silent, watching these two brothers—loving their devotion. Whatever discord had once existed between them was gone. She had no doubt they would die for one another, and perhaps they still might. "May I... give a blessing?" she dared ask.

For a long moment, Wilhelm merely looked at her, frowning, and despite his growing fondness for Rosalynde, she thought he might turn her away, just as he'd refused her healing. Clearly, he still didn't trust her *magik*. But he gave her a nod, and said, "I suspect I shall need all the help I can get."

She gave Giles a wary glance to gauge his reaction, but he, too, nodded, and Rosalynde swept forward, laying a hand on Wilhelm's courser, silently entreating a blessing from the Goddess. "Godspeed," she said, when she was through.

"And to you, my lady," said Wilhelm, giving her a nod, and then another to his lord brother before bolting away.

"Do you think he will fare well alone?"

Giles stood behind her, silent for a moment as the two of them watched Wilhelm go. "My brother is as capable as any," he said, at long last.

It was so much easier to speak her mind with her back to him. "Then perhaps you should say so... he longs for your validation." There was more she longed to say—so much more—but her lips suddenly would not part.

He met her counsel with silence, and the feeling was intensely awkward. And then, after a moment, she started at the feel of a hand gripping her elbow. He drew her back and turned her around to look her into her eyes. "I would rest the night here," he told her.

Rosalynde nodded.

His dark eyes held a silent message. "We have a long journey ahead, and we need rest, but... I prefer not to let you out of my sight."

Rosalynde nodded again, understanding.

"I would explain to Mother Helewys that you are my lady wife."

One last time, Rosalynde nodded, though her

knees felt weak, and her heart beat painfully as she peered up, meeting his deep, dark eyes.

For a long, long moment, they merely stared at one another... and then, he moved closer, and lifted a hand to her cheek, then bent to press a small kiss to her forehead... then another over the bridge of her nose... and there... he allowed his lips to linger, warm and pliant against her already fevered skin.

At last, would they speak of the bonding? Was it possible that he, too, had heard the Goddess?

Rosalynde dared to hope.

After an excruciating moment, he slid a hand to her chin, lifting her face to his gaze... and he gave her one more, firm but chaste brush of his lips... upon the lips, and sweet though it might be, it held a certain promise in its tenderness.

"Can you stand by my side and give credence to my words, Rose?"

She loved the way he said her name—so intimately, and she would do anything he asked of her and more, but she realized it was one thing to stand by whilst Wilhelm offered the ladies of Neasham a handful of glittering gold, and yet another to stand before them in full view of their scrutiny, and answer as his wife.

"Of course," she said, though she worried.

What would happen if the prioress should happen to note her stolen habit? She didn't want to hide anymore—not with any *glamour*. But despite that the woolen material wasn't very fine, the needlework was very distinct, with the sisters' signature embroidery on the sleeves and hem. And still, Rosalynde hadn't the heart to confess as much to Giles. She didn't want him to know the depths of her deceptions, justified though they might be.

Her Welsh grandmother had had a saying for times like these... for times when fate lay beyond the control of mere mortals.

Beth fydd.

Whatever would be, would be.

23

Rosalynde stood meekly by Giles's side whilst he bargained with the prioress, concealing her sleeves and too-short hem beneath her borrowed cloak. Only now she wondered... what might have happened if she'd never stolen the habit?

Would Seren be wed to Giles? Would her sister have returned with him to Warkworth?

As life happened, nothing occurred without consequence—at least that's what Rhi so oft claimed. And here was a perfect example: The nuns at Neasham were world-renowned seamstresses. They sold their services to support their work at the priory, where they hosted an almonry as well as a hospital. Even to the most discerning eye, their needlework was superior, and the Queen Consort oft commissioned their services. And, of course, whatever the Queen had one of her mother must keep twenty. Pride in excess was Morwen's weakness, and she was not immune to vainglory. Therefore, merely so she wouldn't feel humiliated by the poor state of her daughters' dress, she had commissioned three new gowns, one for each. After all, it wouldn't be seemly to allow Henry's offspring—illegitimate though they might be—to be dressed so meanly whilst at court.

And yet, it must also be noted that not once during their years at Llanthony had Morwen ever provided them a single dress—not for twelve long years, even as they'd doubled in height and formed a woman's curves. Rather, the sisters had fashioned their own gowns from cast-off robes. And if, indeed, they had arrived at Westminster in tatters, they had been proud enough to be wearing the fruits of their own labors. But this, of course, was neither here nor there.

Knowing Seren would be paraded before the court during her presentation to the lord of Warkworth, Morwen had commissioned a second dress for Seren. That was when Rosalynde acquired the nun's habit. Having accompanied her sister to the fitting, she'd spied the habit folded in a chair, and when Sister Emma handed Rosalynde their finished stack of gowns, she'd very nonchalantly laid them atop the habit, and when they'd quit her chamber, Rosalynde took the habit as well. After all, it could so easily have been a mistake—or so she would have claimed if someone caught her. But no one did. Essentially, that stolen gown led to her escape, and having fled when she did, she stole the *very* horse of the *very* man her sister had been intended to wed.

And this was the *ysbryd y byd* her sister Rhiannon sometimes spoke of. According to Rhi, life was so much like a spider's web, everything integrally connected. Free will was a gift, but *all* divergent paths led to a shared end—a boundary not unlike the verge of the spider's web, a delicate filament to be plucked like a harp, in tune to a song inspired by the hearts of men. Only whether that song be good or bad, happy or sad, depended on the spirit of the age, the *ysbryd y byd*.

Now what would happen if Mother Helewys happened to note her stolen habit? Would she realize it was Sister Emma's? Would she insist upon knowing the circumstances? Would she glean the truth and then tell Morwen?

To make matters worse, it was only then as she endeavored to hide her stolen garb that she considered the utter humiliation of arriving at Aldergh dressed in her current state—now, in truth, she was in tatters. Her poor sister would fear she'd been assaulted—and, well, so she had, but not under the circumstances Elspeth and her husband might think. But, as luck would have it, she worried for naught. Apparently, the five gold marks they'd offered for Lady Ayleth's soul, plus whatever Giles paid for the room, was more than enough impetus for the prioress to accept his money without question. In fact, she invited them to sup in their hall, though thankfully, Giles declined, with the excuse that they'd been traveling too long, and his *wife* had an ague in her bones. If the prioress had any reservations at all, it was only when Giles ordered the bath. She gave Rose a narrow-eyed glance, though before she could say aught, Giles handed the woman another sterling, and off she went, happily, to do his bidding.

Perhaps she'd feared, as Rosalynde feared, that Giles meant for them to trollop together in the sanctity of her priory, but that too was a needless concern. When the bath arrived, Giles offered her a smile that put a twinkle in his dark eyes, and he left as in marched a procession of nuns, carrying a small tub, buckets, soap, towels, and the last in line held a stack of folded gowns.

"Oh, nay! There must be some mistake," Rose said, peering out the door, but Giles was already gone.

The woman smiled serenely. "Oh, nay, Lady Rosalynde. Your husband procured them." She glanced at the cloak Rose had pinched so jealously, perhaps wondering what lay beneath. "My lord of Warkworth informed us that you met some trouble on the road. For this we are heartily aggrieved." The corners of the nun's eyes crinkled. "For all your generosity, Mother Helewys has also provided her own small gift for your troubles."

Guilt gnawed at Rosalynde's belly.

The woman shook her head sadly. "We've not been able to take our wagons through Darkwood for years now." With a tilt of her head, she thrust out the stack, insisting that Rosalynde take it. "Rife with thieves and cutthroats, and I dare not say what more."

"Thank you," said Rose, shamefaced. And yet it was only after the nun departed that she understood the true generosity of the gifts... There was not one, but two gowns amidst the lot. One of them rivaled the gown her sister had worn to the King's Hall. The first layer was a gold-threaded camlet, fine as the finest silk *chainse*. The surcoat was a thick azure color made of a lovely corded fabric, soft as velvet. The color reminded Rosalynde of bellflowers. There was also a cloak to match in a darker shade of blue, generously trimmed with soft ermine.

Apparently, the *catskin* cloak was no longer amidst their belongings, and later, Giles would tell her the sisters accepted the donation graciously. But, of course, they would; it was a beautiful cloak, if only one didn't know what it was made of.

Supper arrived after her bath, delivered by none other than Giles himself. Anticipating the moment of his arrival, Rosalynde received him dressed in one of her bright new gowns, hoping with all her heart that she'd chosen the one he preferred. After all, it would be their first night alone together and she wanted to thank him properly... and more, she wanted him to know how willingly she came to their union, even if he didn't properly understand the gifts the Goddess had granted them.

Giles froze as he opened the door.

Whatever he had expected to encounter upon returning to the room, he hadn't expected such a brilliant transformation. But it was more than the dress. As a matter of confession, he had been anticipating seeing her again, dressed in something more appropriate to her station, but nothing could have prepared him for the smile she bestowed upon him as he entered the room. It glowed more brightly than his sword ever could, and, in response, like an untried youth, he nearly dropped the tray he held.

Her hair was freshly washed and plaited, her skin translucent, and without the wimple, veil and filth, he could see every detail all-too clearly.

She was... breathtaking.

She was... precisely the woman he'd envisioned in his dreams. His siren...

She was... heartrendingly beautiful... her nose pert and sweet. Her lips so full and rosy. Her hair full of shimmer, catching the copper gleam of firelight. And her eyes shone with the light of an inner flame.

"You look... beautiful," he said, averting his gaze, as he moved toward the room's only table to set down the tray.

"*You* are beautiful, my lord," she said, with a tremble in her voice, and Giles chuckled softly, very swiftly losing all his good sense. God have mercy, it was all he could do not to strip the lady bare and lay her down upon that well-made bed, peel away her *chainse* and replace the garment with his burning lips... alas, he would not.

No matter that they seemed to have formed some inexplicable bond, she was still a lady, whose honor must be defended... including from himself.

Particularly from himself.

Alas, he could not explain his sense of duty to her. But then, nothing about this past week was even remotely explicable. She was Morwen Pendragon's daughter—a witch by her own admission. Giles was a Paladin, sworn to eradicate her kind from this earth.

And yet... there was naught about Rosalynde Pendragon that was evil, and even now his sword lay silent against the wall where he'd put it... which was more than he could say about his other *sword*.

Gods' truth, if there was any witchery at play here, it was only this: His heart would not stop thumping in her presence and his lungs felt too constricted to breathe. His blood simmered through his veins and his cock stirred against his will.

She was nervous, he could tell. He could see that she stood trembling, like a bride on her first night, with hands joined primly together, and her alabaster cheeks the color of a rose in bloom—a rose in winter.

For all that he might be twice her age, he was nervous, too—a fact that bewildered him. What was she? Twenty perhaps? He was thirty-three, yet, through his service in the Guard, he felt twice that.

Even when he'd first laid eyes upon her beautiful sister, he hadn't felt this way—even knowing that she was meant to lie beneath him. He had never once looked at Seren Pendragon as anything more than a Morwen spy—an agent for his ruin.

Now, in truth, if he must confess this fact—if only to himself—he hadn't felt this confused by any woman since his first blush—not since Lady Ayleth. And even then, he never felt this... overwhelming desire to claim her for his own... to put his seed in her belly. He wanted to imagine her with his daughters at her skirts and his son suckling at her bosom...

As profane as it might seem... he wanted to suckle there himself...

And yet he was already betrothed, and this was no matter he could easily resolve—not when so many people depended upon the success of his charade.

At least for the time being, he must not embrace the way he felt. Later perhaps... but only perhaps.

And regardless, she must be famished—as famished as he was for the velvety sweetness of her skin.

"Thank you," she said, and he struggled to recover himself, removing the twin goblets from the tray he'd brought. Taking his time, settlings his thoughts, he placed them on the table, and then picked up the flagon, intending to indulge himself until his mutinous cock could no longer stir.

At any rate, his mouth felt entirely too parched...

"WOULD YOU LIKE SOME *VIN*?" he asked, clearing his throat, and when Rosalynde didn't immediately reply, he gestured toward the goblets.

"Yeah... please... thank you, my lord."

My lord... the words sounded oddly formal in this richly adorned bower, when all week long he had been merely Giles, and they'd slept scandalously close, even sharing one blanket. And yet, in all that time, it had never once occurred to Rose to be embarrassed by their proximity—not even with her ruined gown. It wasn't in her nature to be self-conscious. Only now, she felt painfully shy for the first time in her life, and she averted her gaze, examining the room.

Unlike the rest of the nunnery, the guest rooms were well fitted, if modestly so, with soft linens and sapphire blue curtains hanging from irons above a small, high window.

It wasn't particularly a surprise, for despite that these nuns created such beautiful fabrics and gowns, Sister Emma herself had worn the simplest of dresses. The priory was the same—humble for the women who dwelt here, but snug and fit for their guests.

It was late now; the sun was already setting. Its rays impaled the leaded glass—not so fine as the *waldglas* at Llanthony, and yet beautiful anyway, separating the sun's hues over the white-sheeted bed—violet, blue, red, green, gold.

Beside the simple canopy, a small brazier burned very low, but still hot enough to warm the room. Alas, to Rosalynde's dismay, it seemed that all its warmth crept into her cheeks.

Freshly scrubbed from her bath, she felt naked, exposed, even despite the lovely gown she wore. There was no wimple to hide the red of her hair, no veil to hide the trembling of her lips—nor, for that matter, any *glamour* spell to hide her true face. She was precisely who—and what—she was, and if she must be judged by her looks alone, she would never, ever measure up to her sister.

And still, she dared to hope... if only because of the look Giles gave her as he came through the door... as though she must be the most beautiful maiden in all the realm. He was still gazing at her that way...

His gaze never left her as he poured the *vin* in both their goblets, and then he set the flagon down again, and once he was through, he lifted one goblet for Rosalynde to take. He gave her a heart-tripping smile, as he said, in jest, "To our continued ability to breathe."

"I suppose 'tis one way to put it," Rosalynde said, laughing softly, taking the goblet.

"And how else would you put it, *Sister Rosalynde?*"

Sister Rosalynde.

Her gaze shot up, only to realize he must be teasing her—for the first time ever, and now that he dared to her cheeks grew warmer still. Embarrassed, because she had ever meant to deceive him, Rosalynde lifted her glass, returning his smile. "Alas," she protested. "I haven't a gift for words, my lord."

He lifted a golden brow, his lips curving ever-so slyly. "To my knowledge, Lady Rosalynde, you've never had a loss for any words," he said, and her face burned hotter, until she felt the flush ignite her bosom. "And nevertheless," he said. "Never fear, as it seems to me you have more than your share of gifts already—not the least of which is your smile."

Rosalynde's heart tripped wildly.

Very shyly, she lifted her goblet to her lips, grateful for the sweet elixir to calm her nerves—and Goddess please, she planned to drink a *lot* tonight, if only so she could forget that she meant to lie with her sister's intended.

And no matter... she knew in her heart that Seren would be the first to sanction this union. Seren was not capable of envy, and neither could she possibly have any affection for Giles de Vere—not like Rose did. After all, how could anyone endure such trials and not be bonded?

Unbidden, the Goddess's words came back to tease her, and she flushed hotly, because if those words were not imagined... if, in truth, they were to be believed... they must already be wed in the eyes of the

Goddess... and still... not once had Giles dared to acknowledge what had happened.

Rose understood that he must not have experienced them. Such things were not meant for the ears of common men—and yet, he was hardly, in the true sense of the word... common.

Whatever the case, she had no compunction about what she was about to do—none at all. She had been taught to revel in all that made her a woman. Her ancestors had been pagans, who, instead of being ashamed of the act of procreation, had been taught that the creation of life was the greatest gift to be bestowed upon the world, and if she could thank Giles, she would thank him with her body and her soul.

Only what she felt for him was more than gratitude. She felt something deeper. She felt... *love*, for what was love after all, but a higher form of *magik*, born of faith, trust and devotion?

When all was said and done, it wasn't just that Giles was the first man she'd ever known so intimately. It wasn't merely that he was also the most beautiful man she'd ever known. Nor was it only that she'd spent so many hours reveling in the warmth of his embrace. And nay, it wasn't because he'd saved her life. She liked *him,* truly. She liked *everything* about him. She liked the way he ate. She loved his smile. She loved the way he walked and talked. She loved the quiet strength and power he wielded so easily. She loved the patience he showed his brother, and most of all, she loved the way he made her feel...

He gestured toward the table, and Rosalynde's knees buckled as she moved closer to discover that he'd brought her a bit of mutton, cheese and bread. In truth, she wasn't very hungry, but she knew she must try—else the *vin* would go straight to her head, and she wanted desperately that tonight should be divine...

"Forgive me," he said. "I ate. All save the *vin* is for you."

Rose's hand fluttered to her breast. "For me?"

She was overcome with emotion. It wasn't enough that he would buy her gowns and then deign to serve her, but not even at Westminster had she dined so finely. Not for one minute was her mother ever concerned about *how* her daughters filled their bellies, much less *what* they ate. And so much as they had been surrounded by opulence at the palace, they would have preferred Llanthony with their crude dirt floors. At least then they could have eaten from their garden. But this—she swept her hand reverently over the laden tray. It was too much to eat alone, and what was worse, as famished as she should have been, she had inexplicably lost her appetite. There was a fluttering in her belly, like a hundred thousand angels flittering all at once.

Retrieving her hand, she put it about her cup, bringing the goblet slowly to her lips. "I shall eat later," she promised with a smile, as he watched her, all the while twirling his own cup in his hand.

What should she do now?

Rosalynde turned to regard the bed, wondering what should come next... the room was so warm now that she could easily undress... and rush into the bed.

"How is your wound?" he asked.

"Healed," she reassured him. "But... I do have scars." And her blush returned as she considered that she must now reveal all her imperfections.

And yet—she furrowed her brow—she was quite puzzled, because, truly, she had never known a healing spell not to remove wound marks as well. She now had eight hideous black pocks that were clearly visible, even after a week—not unlike the darkening scars that Wilhelm now wore on his face.

"And this surprises you?"

Rosalynde nodded. "Perhaps," she confessed, but then... she didn't know what else to say.

Now should she undress and get into the bed?

What must he think of her compared to her sister?

Behind her, Giles sank into one of the chairs. And then he sat for such an excruciatingly long while, facing the bed. In fact, he waited so long to speak that, outside, full darkness descended, bathing the room in shadows. On the bed, the rainbow prism vanished, and still, he sipped quietly at his *vin*...

What if, after all, he didn't want her? What if, in truth, Rose imagined everything? What if the bond she felt was nothing more than a heartfelt wish?

Feeling compelled to, she now returned to the table, forcing herself to pick up a piece of the bread, taking a nibble. "'Tis good," she said, and thanked him again, acutely aware that his eyes never left her, until, at long last, he broached the subject they'd been so studiously avoiding all week long, and she felt a terrible prick of dread.

"You must know, Rose... I am betrothed to your sister?"

"I-I do, my lord." Rosalynde's heart thudded to a halt.

A deeper silence fell between them... a silence that brought the sizzling inside the brazier to a roar, and Rosalynde forced herself to take another bite of the bread, making herself chew.

"As God is my witness, I do not care about the title, and yet... if I do not honor my contract with Stephen, I stand to lose Warkworth."

Rosalynde's throat constricted. The bread inside her mouth turned to paste, and her heart squeezed painfully.

Somehow, she had not considered *him* in this, but... yeah, of course. He stood to lose everything... and why did she think he was only here to serve the will of Goddess?

"I made a bargain," he said. "My fealty to Stephen for the chance to rebuild... and... to seal our deal, I accepted your sister's hand. Our wedding is to be six months hence."

"I wouldst..." Rosalynde shook her head, setting the rest of the bread down, losing what little appetite she had mustered. She lifted her hand to her mouth, perhaps to keep herself from retching, and with much, much effort, she managed to swallow what she had in her mouth, then, she lifted her goblet, along with the flagon, pouring from its contents until her goblet was full to the brim. "I... I do... not... wish to see you lose Warkworth... my lord." She set the flagon down, very quietly.

"If it were only me..."

Rosalynde would have lifted a hand if she could, but both of them were strangling her goblet. "You need not explain," she said, tipping the goblet to her lips, draining the contents. "So, then... you would still wed my sister, Seren?"

"That... is the plan," he said, and Rose's eyes filled with hot tears she daren't shed. With shaking hands, she poured another goblet full and then once again tipped it to her lips, gulping until she was no longer in danger of weeping. "My sister... Seren is wonderful," she said, swallowing her grief. "You will love her."

He said naught to that, and until that instant, Rosalynde hadn't ever dared begrudge her sisters aught.

24

room was a prison, and yet, it was not.

The window might have bars, and the door
locked, but the brazier burned hot and
nd the woodpile was tall—taller than any
er had at Llanthony.

was more, there was no longer any need to
she was... She was a *dewine*, a child of the
ther, a student of the *hud*. There was
be had in that, even as her body remained
d.

e, the moon rose high, bathing her in its sil-
It was long, long past the Golden Hour, but
rong now—strong enough not to need the
en times to fortify her *magik*.

rom the bed—a finely curtained bed, thick
rs, not straw to fatten the mattress—Rhi-
ed across the room, lifting up a good-sized
rried it back to the brazier, pushing it into
y.

igh, she reached into her pocket, and took
os she'd separated, tossing them gingerly
giving them a moment to burn. Finally,
ready, she spoke the words.

Only now that she knew Giles... now that they had
shared so much together... the very thought of Seren
wedding him seemed a sore, sore lack of grace on the
part of the Goddess.

Something like anger ignited in her breast, for
how could she provide Rosalynde a champion, only to
wrest him away and return him to her beautiful sister?

It wasn't fair.

"You mustn't worry, Rose. I gave you my word to
see you safely to Aldergh, and this I'll do. As luck
would have it, whilst I'm there, I have business to address with your sister's husband."

Rosalynde nodded once, wanting to ask what business a dutiful earl could have with a traitor to the
crown, but her tongue was too thick to speak. Swallowing her grief, she turned away, refusing to meet his
gaze. "I... I am not hungry, after all," she said as she
moved toward the bed, suddenly, feeling more ener-
vated than she had even on the day she'd faced
Mordecai.

Goddess help her, for all that she'd felt a sense of
purpose in regard to the *grimoire*, it suddenly seemed a
terrible, terrible waste—not for the rest of the realm
perhaps, but, for her. Without Giles, it felt as though
her world had already ended. But how could that be
so? "Thank you... *so* much... for all you've done, my
lord. If you would pardon me now, I should desperately like to sleep."

"I understand," he said, watching her tear down
the bedding. "Don't worry, my lady," he said formally.
"I intended to sleep in this chair."

Rose's brows slanted sadly. "Of course," she said,
and crawled into the bed, pulling the covers high over
her head, not caring that she might wrinkle her fabu-
lous new gown. She didn't want Giles to see her tear-

stricken face, and she wished so much that she still had her wimple and veil.

Yeah, she was angry, embarrassed, disappointed. Sad. And all these things shouldn't have mattered, because, after all, he was still helping her with the *one* thing she *most* needed... getting the *grimoire* to Elspeth.

Everything else was all but fantasy.

It didn't matter, she told herself.

Nothing mattered.

She didn't need him.

And yet, she did.

Giles tossed down another gulp of the *vin*, and sweet as the taste might be, it was bitter on his tongue.

Rosalynde's emotions were honest and without guile. He could tell that he had hurt her, and it sorely aggrieved him.

They had been inseparable since the ordeal in the glade, but he was losing his resolve, as swiftly as he was losing his religion. Rosalynde Pendragon was *not* for him, and he mustn't confuse the mission he'd embarked upon. His sword belonged to the Church, even if his heart now belonged to a beauteous witch... a witch, in truth.

And that, too, was a cross to be borne... because he no more intended to kill the lady, than he meant to bed her. Instead, he would be her advocate to the Church. He would make certain they understood she was not her mother.

For the longest time, he sat, watching the poor girl sleep, feeling more exhausted and confused than he had in all his years. More than aught, he wanted to go to her, comfort her, make love to her... make her his own.

But... he'd had plenty of time to reconsider his

folly, and simply because he'd d didn't mean he was meant to ha could simply have been God's way that her plight was not to be ignor

Or, it could be a warning, b she had been a water nymph—a the depths of the sea, who'd lur and perhaps to hell itself.

In truth, if he forsook his would put in danger all the Chu

And, more... in his selfish both his brothers, his father, a of all, England.

He could not risk it. How helm if he returned to War Pendragon by his side and it

Nay. He could not take I longed to and his body could not.

Blazing fires as you dance,
Give me now a fleeting glance.

A puff of smoke lifted from the brazier, the scent like burnt honey. The wisps and curls took shape, forming, forming... forming...

She didn't need the fire, or words anymore, but she reveled in the rites her people had performed for ages.

Still, her face fell, and her brows slanted at what was revealed to her, and her heart wrenched so painfully that she thought she might howl at the moon.

Goddess please... it was the most impossible decision for any sister to make—to choose one to lose.

Encourage one to a given path, and it sent the other to her doom.

Few things in life were only coincidences. No happenstance occurred without consequence.

If only people understood that there was a price to be paid for every thought that formed and every decision made, they might tremble in their boots.

Her lips trembled as she fought her desire to weep... how utterly impossible a decision... *help one, lose two. Help two, lose one.* And if it could be possible to sacrifice herself, she would do so without hesitation... but this would not change the fates. Even without a scrying stone, even without *mindspeaking*, she knew where Seren and Arwyn were. She understood the decision Rosalynde must make, and she knew what it would cost.

And yet... no matter how many times she twisted and turned the *aether*, there was only *one* true path that would return their mother to the place whence she'd come.

Goddess save them, she knew the truth; it was

more terrifying than anyone could imagine: Morwen was not her grandmamau's child—not any longer. In her greed for power and glory, she had brought forth a demon from the Nether Realm—a soul that should not have found its way back to the dominion of men. She was *not* Morwen, daughter of Morgan Pendragon. She was *not* a child of Taliesin... she was the witch who'd sought the prophet's doom. She was Cerridwen, destroyer of realms, called back to this world by a blood *magik* so hideous that by its very act, the veil between worlds had rent but long enough for Cerridwen to escape, and after thousands and thousands of years trapped in her black prison, she would stop at naught to see vengeance done.

For a long, long moment, Rhiannon dared to grieve for the little girl who'd once been her mother... the child who'd lamented her faults... the young lady who'd envied her mother's affection for her elder brother, the last warlock of their age. Emrys Pendragon had been his mother's pride and joy—even as Cerridwen had loved her own son, Morfran. Except, Emrys was not cursed as Morfran had been cursed. He was blessed, as the sisters were blessed, by the blood of Taliesin. Emrys Pendragon, *not* Morwen, was the regnant priest of their age, and Rhiannon knew it... because... Emrys was her father. Murdered by her mother... even as Morwen had murdered Rhiannon's twin in her own womb.

She'd poisoned him.

Rage burned hot as the embers in her brazier, and she swore that one day she would avenge them *all*, even as she must avenge the sister who must now die by her own judgment...

Grief twisted her heart, curdling in her belly, and she didn't care who heard her cry. She wanted to curl into a ball, and somehow cease to exist, but that was not the way of a regnant priestess.

Heartsore, she returned to the bed, and sat upon it another long while, burdened by the weight of her duty. The bed creaked beneath her, and she heard the shuffle of feet outside her prison door.

He was there... again... but she didn't care.

And neither did she care if her mother overheard her. If she hesitated, the moment will have passed.

It *must* be tonight, else he would harden his heart, and so, too, would Rosalynde, and if their union was not consummated, the consequences would not be theirs alone.

Rosalynde, she called through the *aether*. *Sister hear me.* And she closed her eyes, easily infiltrating Rosalynde's thoughts as her sister lay weeping... her eyes red-rimmed and sore. "Stop," she whispered softly. "Dry your eyes, my dear." And then she hardened her voice. "We are not born to weep for our sins, we are here to honor the Goddess with our gifts. You have a duty to fulfill."

"Rhiannon?"

"Aye, 'tis me, Rose, but there's no time to explain. Bind him to you. You know how. The Goddess has ordained it. Seren will understand. Trust your heart to do what is right... as you have always done."

Silence.

One tear slid from her amber eyes, trickling onto the richly adorned bed as she repeated the words of the Goddess.

> Bound by destiny, to destiny bound,
> Another to one, and one to another...

Outside her door, she heard a man's rueful laughter. Then she heard a slam of his fist against the stone wall, and his footfalls fell away.

Let him go... in the end, the Goddess's will must be done... even in regard to *him*.

❧

ROSALYNDE HAD BEEN HALF ASLEEP, dozing fitfully, her eyes swollen with tears, but she awoke with a start.

> Bound by destiny, to destiny bound,
> Another to one, and one to another...

Those were precisely the words she'd heard the glade, and her sister betimes knew things. As a child Rosalynde had learned to trust Rhiannon, even when Elspeth had constrained them.

Inhaling a breath for courage, she shoved the blanket off her head to find the night was late and the moon was high, silver light washing into the room.

For all that he mustn't be comfortable, Giles was nevertheless sleeping, because she heard his smooth, even breathing. She did not let that dissuade her, rising from the bed, her feet instinctively taking her where she needed to go... without having sensed she'd moved them.

Bind him to you. You know how.

Aye, she did know, because she was a woman, and it was a knowledge all women carried in their heart of hearts.

The goblet lay empty in his hand. The flagon, she sensed, was empty as well. Perhaps emboldened by the elixir herself, she stared at the man her heart was coming to know and love...

She wanted more than simply to do her duty to the

Goddess. She wanted to give him babes. She wanted to feel them quicken in her womb and know she'd conceived them in love.

And yet, for the longest time, she could not move, only stare...

In slumber his swarthy face was no less beautiful. In the shadows, his blond hair was dark about the jaw, but the firelight made it glisten... like stars.

If he awoke now, would he see her lithe body illumined by the fire, even through her gown? Would he note her nipples straining against the *chainse*, only longing for lips to suckle? Would he tremble over the desire he would spy in her eyes?

Before she could stop herself, she lifted the delicate *chainse* he'd bought, and pulled it gently over her head, tossing it on the floor, next to his sword and scabbard. One by one, she shed her inhibitions even as she shed her garments, allowing herself to be vulnerable and exposed. And, then, when she was ready, she bent with trembling hands to pry the goblet from his fingers. He opened his eyes as she placed it on the table, and the sound it made was like the clink of a coin...

Giles blinked away the sleep from his eyes, afraid he must be dreaming... But, nay... there she was, naked and unashamed, standing before him with nary a stitch of clothes—and God help him, he was only a man, a man with no will left at all.

"If, in truth, I must lose you to my sister," she said softly, tears shining in her eyes. "I will have you once, to keep the memory in my heart." He watched a tear slip from her eye and roll down her cheek, off her chin, onto her hardened nipple, glistening like molten silver. The sight of it nearly unmanned him where he sat, and despite the *vin*, his cock hardened, aching for the touch of her hand.

She was a siren, leading him to his doom, and he did not care right now. Every nerve in his body lit, and his gaze fixed on the eight small wounds she'd received in the glade, revealed now by the light of the moon... His heart twisted, and his lips longed to ease them... But, alas, he could not blame it on the *vin* when he lifted his hands to her waist, holding her fast, pulling himself forward to lay his burning mouth upon her scars, kissing them each in turn, lapping them one by one with his tongue, as though he might somehow erase the burdens from her flesh.

She shivered, but not with fear, he realized, as he peered up into her beautiful violet eyes. The desire he saw there was his undoing and he shuddered as he felt his own wetness, a small bead of his seed soak into the cloth of his breeches.

"Rosalynde," he said thickly. "You cannot know what it is you are asking."

She nodded but once, firmly, and said, "I do, my lord."

And still, though he ached with desire, he slid a hand to her belly, soft as silk, pushing her back. "You need not thank me for my services, Rosalynde. And yet... if you test me, I am sure to disappoint you."

She reached down, putting a trembling hand over his, both their hands now quaking—only hers with trepidation. Only his with desire, and all his body shook with it, even as the blood rushed to his cock, filling it so thickly that it throbbed.

"Rosalynde," he said again, one last protest, and she answered by guiding his hand lower, into the velvety mons between her thighs.

It was all Giles could do not to spill his seed where

he sat. Swallowing with difficulty, he rose from the chair, undressing, never taking his eyes off Rosalynde, letting her know... if she didn't want him—want this—she'd best say so now. But she said naught, and off came his *sherte*, then his breeches. He hurled them both aside with a ferocity that startled even him, and then he stood before her as naked and unashamed as she... fully revealed by the light of a full moon.

When still she said nothing, only gasped very softly, he smiled darkly and slid an arm about her waist, pulling her close, letting her feel the unyielding hardness of his body, and all his pent-up desire.

Rosalynde's breath caught at the feel of him—his manhood, thick and insistent against her thighs, teasing her, even of its own accord. And, for the longest moment, he stood, allowing her to feel him, as though willing her to deny him. But, she would not...

> Bound by destiny, to destiny bound,
> Another to one, and one to another...

And still... she didn't know what to do. She was a virgin still. Only when she thought her heart would rend in two, he bent to press a kiss upon the bridge her nose... then another on her mouth, opening his mouth as though he meant to devour her, and then sliding out his tongue to brush against her trembling mouth. She opened her lips to him—like a flower opening to the warmth of the sun—and moaned softly as his tongue slipped inside, tasting her so intimately that she thought she might die. She pushed him away, if only to say, "I shall never take another lover."

"I cannot ask that of you," he said, pulling away, but Rose clung to him, not allowing it. She slid her arms about him, holding him close, letting him feel the hardness of her own nipples against his flesh, even as he'd teased her with his own flesh.

"It does not matter," she said. "I will love you always. And tonight, at least... I am yours."

He growled then, and said naught more, lifting her up and carrying Rosalynde to the bed...

25

ALDERGH CASTLE, FEBRUARY 1149

There were flurries in the air, white, plump, and dancing with all the promise of winter. And nevertheless, peppered in snow though she might be, Rosalynde wasn't cold, nor had she any need for warming spells or layers of clothes whilst Giles held her so jealously. Even so, she shivered, excited to see her sister, Elspeth.

Looming before her, like a patchwork dragon on its haunches, Aldergh was a monstrosity. From end to end, it must be at least ten-thousand meters long, and evidently, it was built in stages, judging by the multicolored stone and the varied design. Behind it, she could spy the dusky rose foothills of the Pennines, dusted in a fresh layer of snow.

"Art cold?" Giles asked, though he didn't wait for an answer. He shifted his cloak, so it covered more of Rosalynde than it did of him. And she smiled gratefully, her heart thumping madly.

"I am not cold," she said. "But I am... excited. And perhaps... relieved." For weeks now they had been preparing for the worst, fearfully watching over their shoulders. Mercifully, Morwen never arrived, and

Giles's strange serpentine sword remained silent by his side. For three long weeks they'd traveled under cloak, armed with daggers, and now... here they were... at long last.

By now, Wilhelm, too, must have reached his destination and perhaps he was already preparing defenses, but there was no way to know for sure.

Rhiannon, too, remained quiet since that night at Neasham, and Rosalynde dared not entreat her. Somehow, her sister's *magik* was powerful enough to reach across the *aether*, but hers was not, and she daren't tempt Morwen.

"Soon now," Giles promised, and it was a promise he could easily keep, because they were here now, and neither snow, hail, nor Morwen Pendragon could stop them.

Giles halted for a moment, so they could admire the fortress—the soaring corner towers and the thick curtain wall, expansive enough to protect an entire village. And yet, though it was immense and quite impressive, it couldn't be considered beautiful, with the mishmash of stone and design. But it was a bulwark, to be sure—a deterrence to men who would defy its lord, and, if it could be safe anywhere, the *grimoire* would be safe here.

And nevertheless, as big as the castle was, it was impossible to imagine her sister had somehow managed to cast a protection spell around its perimeter to shield her people. Once again Rose wished she had been there to witness it—and moreover, she wished she could have seen her mother's face as she'd watched from afar. Even now, Morwen was lamenting the loss of her birds, and it would take years and years and years to replace them.

"Someday, I shall see Warkworth inviolable," Giles

told her, squeezing her gently, and Rosalynde smiled, because someday, she, too, hoped to see his beloved home. No matter how small, or how grand, she would love it, because it belonged to Giles de Vere.

Up on the ramparts, men scurried between machicolations, the silver in their armor winking defiantly against the midday sun. Rosalynde sat in awe whilst snowflakes tickled her nose and settled like cold dust in her hair.

"Ready?" he asked

"Aye," she said, nodding, as she gripped the small pommel with white-knuckled fists and Giles set a heel to the courser's hind. As they approached, a single horn-blast trumpeted across the field and her heart pummeled against her ribs.

A warning? A greeting?

Alas, they had no pennant to show, but Giles neither quickened his pace, nor did he slow. He held the trot, until they sat waiting before the castle gates, and then he called to the gatekeeper.

"Who goes there?" asked the man.

"Giles of Warkworth," he said. "I come bearing the Lady Rosalynde Pendragon to see her sister, the lady of Aldergh."

Silence met his declaration, and after a moment of consideration, the gatekeeper asked, "Can you prove it, lord? We have orders to admit no one."

"Call your lord," Giles demand. "I would speak to him."

"Nay," said the man. "I will not."

"Will not or cannot?" asked Giles.

The man remained silent, appraising Giles and Rosalynde with suspicious eyes.

Without a word, Giles swept the cloak off Rosalynde's shoulders, impatiently showing the man his sigil

—a lion sejant holding in his dexter-paw an axe, and in the sinister, a tilting-spear.

The man replied, "These are lawless days, lord. I hear Warkworth lies in ruins—its lord murdered. Could be you took the cloak from his dead body."

Up on the ramparts, the sound of men nocking their bows reached their ears, and Rosalynde peered up to see that there were fifty men or more, ready to loose arrows.

"Have you more proof, lord? If not, I am compelled to keep my lord's command. As you have probably surmised, the safety of my lady is my burden."

"I *am* Giles de Vere," he countered, prepared to argue his case. "*Earl* of Warkworth—"

"Wait," Rosalynde bade him. She lifted a hand to Giles and then her head to the guardsman and smiled.

She heard the frown in his voice as Giles whispered in her ear. "My dear, as beauteous as your smile may be, I cannot think it will persuade the man. He sounds like a dungeon master I knew."

"Just you wait," she advised.

Mindspeaking was not something she did so well with anyone but her sisters, but she had no doubt Elspeth could hear her now that she was in proximity. Despite the lord of Warkworth's acceptance of her *dewinity*, she was careful not to overburden him. So, of course, she didn't tell him what she was doing, and for a long, long moment, there was no answer—none at all. And suddenly, when Rose feared they might be turned away after all, she heard a voice shouting behind the gates and a smile broke on her face from ear to ear. *Elspeth.* No matter how long since she'd last heard her eldest sister's voice, Rosalynde would always recognize it. It was the voice of the one person in this world who'd sung to her as a babe... who'd scrubbed her ears and brushed her hair.

"Open the gates!" Elspeth demanded. "Open the gates!" And, without argument, the heavy portcullis began to rise, straining against its ancient chains.

Rosalynde turned to Giles. "See what you can do with a little kindness, my lord?"

26

Never in her life could Rosalynde have guessed that halloos could be as heart-rending as good-byes, but now she knew, as she stood clutching her eldest sister, her throat tight and hot tears burning her eyes.

It had been far too long—ten long, long months to be precise, and in the meantime, so much had transpired.

Elspeth, too, seemed overcome—the moisture pooling in her eyes dampening the crook of Rosalynde's neck.

Forsooth, she had somehow forgotten how diminutive Elspeth was, and lest she be mistaken, there was a bit more flesh on her bones as well. She squeezed her sister desperately. And then, finally, after the two had stood so long that their audience began to look about awkwardly, they wrenched themselves apart, to look into one another's red-rimmed eyes. "I cannot believe 'tis you," exclaimed Elspeth, her violet-blue eyes twinkling with joy.

Rosalynde swallowed a lump that rose in her throat. "Yeah, 'tis me," she said, overjoyed. "And wedlock has clearly been good to you, Elspeth."

Elspeth's lips curled into a secret grin. "Aye, well, as to that... I have something to show you." And she took Rosalynde by the hand, pulling her toward the *donjon*, abandoning everyone else in the yard.

Rosalynde went, only because Giles tipped her a nod when she turned to seek his gaze. He stood, smiling as he tugged off his gauntlets, encouraging Rosalynde to go. Her very last glimpse of the man who'd risked so much to escort her to safety was of him standing, with his cloak turned over his arm, beneath a swirl of snow and surrounded by Aldergh's men at arms. She wanted desperately to stop Elspeth and go back, but her sister was insistent—and far stronger than she remembered.

Inside the castle, Aldergh was not so elaborate in design as Westminster Palace, and in so many ways, not so fine as Llanthony's chapel, but the northern stronghold was sturdy and well fitted. There were tapestries hanging on most of the walls, and fresh rushes on the floors, the rooms clean as a bone after Willhelm got through with one. In this place, there appeared to be nothing her sister was lacking—not even a proper cauldron as she discovered in the lady's solar. Snuggled in a great hearth there, the pot sat very prominently displayed, with an ever-ready fire burning beneath its belly. And this, she assumed, must be the thing her sister wanted to show her—but nay, they had no sooner laid eyes upon the cauldron, when Elspeth dragged her back out of the room, whisking her through the halls.

There were stone and bronze effigies throughout, many in nooks, and a brazier burning in every room. Servants bustled to and fro, carrying on the household chores, but it was Elspeth who commanded them, with her heavy ring of chatelaine's keys dangling at her belt.

"I can't wait to show you my garden," she said, gushing. "Sadly, there isn't much in it right now, for all the snow."

"I can't wait to see it," said Rosalynde, feeling bewildered, because her sister was the same as she'd always been, but so very different. The Elspeth she had lived with in Llanthony had not been so much a wilting flower, but she had not been so confident either. How could she be? She had lived her entire life afeared for the consequences of her actions—and not only for her own sake.

Here, she called out commands as she passed. "Please make certain the guest quarters are tended," she told one servant as they passed, and the lady nodded and rushed away to do her bidding.

She passed another and said. "Ellyn, please go see that the kitchen has been apprised of our guests."

"Yeah, m'lady!" said the young woman, and she too, flew away in a rush.

"That is Cora's daughter," Elspeth explained, scarcely aware that her every word was met with reverence. In such short time, her sister had created for herself a haven.

"Cora?"

Elspeth smiled. "The steward's wife. She is my housekeeper and my dearest friend. I do not know what I would do without her. Alas, we've only just returned, and the house has been in disarray for months in our absence. We spent the winter in Chreagach Mhor, you see." She cast a glance over her shoulder to be sure Rosalynde was listening.

"Chreagach Mhor?"

"Scotia—near the foothills, where my lord was born."

Rosalynde could scarce take her eyes off the rich, colorful tapestries placed high on the walls, depicting terrible battles. Some of the figures wore a Scot's manner of dress, others wore armor. Still others were depictions of swarthy strangers from faraway lands.

Elspeth smiled, noting the direction of her gaze. "Lovely, to be sure, but, alas, they serve more than to please the eye. This part of the castle was built during the Roman days, much like Blackwood. The walls are not always so sound as they should be to weather the winters. If you listen closely—particularly in my solar —you can hear the howl of the wind through stone and mortar."

"Not so much unlike our cottage at Llanthony, eh? Sometimes I miss those days," said Rosalynde, sadly. "As poor as we were, life was simpler then."

And even as pleased as she was for her sister's good fortune, tears pricked at her eyes, and she planted her heels to recover her emotions. Elspeth spun to face her, her sweet blue eyes full of concern. It took Rosalynde a long moment to find her voice. "As you must know, I am not come for pleasure."

"Of course, I suspected," Elspeth said, and with a sigh, she took Rosalynde's hands in hers, warming them. It was a familiar gesture that Rosalynde had sorely missed. Only Elspeth had ever lavished motherly affection on her this way—loving her, reassuringly.

God forbid Morwen should ever do so. "Our mother is a demon," Rose said, in case Elspeth did not realize.

"I know. Believe me, I know."

Rosalynde felt her throat thickening, again. Only

when she could, there, in the hall, she explained all about the *grimoire*... and the perilous journey she had embarked upon. She told her sister about the Shadow Beast that bore Mordecai's face. She told her about having stolen Giles's horse in London, and Seren's betrothal to the lord of Warkworth. Skipping over the night at Neasham she told her about the night of Morwen's arrival at Llanthony and the atrocities their mother committed at Darkwood.

"She swept into our cottage like a cold, bitter wind, put us on our knees and railed at us for being ingrates. All the while, Ersinius stood smirking as we knelt, choking on our tears. Once she was through, the windbag sent in two guards to escort Rhiannon out the door."

Elspeth's brow furrowed. "Did they perchance take her to Blackwood?"

"How did you know?"

"Malcom spoke to her."

"When?"

"It doesn't matter," Elspeth said, patting Rosalynde's hand, and whatever joy she'd had twinkling in her familiar eyes, it was gone now, at least for the moment.

"We cannot allow Morwen to retrieve the book," Rosalynde said, and she brought a hand to her breast. "In my heart of hearts, I know that book is crucial, and I am as certain of that fact as Rhi was the day she bade you leave us at the priory."

Fat tears swelled in her sister's eyes; one slid past her lashes, then rolled down her cheek. "I am so... so... sorry," she said, taking both of Rosalynde's hands, and folding them together, covering them with her own. "I would have returned if I could... and yet... I did send Malcom to find you." She peered down at her blue-slippered feet. "You were gone."

Rosalynde nodded. "We were gone by first light. Ersinius, for all his pandering to the Church, is her willing servant. He does her bidding no matter what cost. I dare not imagine what treachery they have planned together. But, alas, she has agents across the realm, including the Count of Mortain, and that stupid fool burned Warkworth by her behest— burned it to the ground."

Elspeth's eyes grew round with ill-concealed horror. "Is that not the lord you traveled with?"

Rosalynde nodded.

"Does he know you are Morwen's daughter?"

Rosalynde nodded again and squeezed her sister's hand. "Eustace must *not* be confirmed, Elspeth, and if you have any way to send word to Matilda, you must warn her. He is a villain, no less than our mother, and you were right... we must not turn blind eyes to the truth."

"I have dealt with that man; well I know it."

"So we heard. And yet mother would endeavor to convince everyone you are not here of your own free will."

Elspeth's face flushed. "Rest assured, my sweet sister. So much as I loathe being apart from you, there is nowhere in this world I would rather be. Malcom is..." She inhaled deeply. "Blood of my blood, bone of my bone. He is The One the Goddess ordained for me, and I love him to the depths of my soul." But then, Elspeth looked momentarily away, as though she feared the answer to her next question. "Pray tell, how are Seren and Arwyn?"

Rosalynde shook her head sadly. "I do not know. They were well enough when I left London, but Morwen..."

"Say no more." Elspeth patted Rosalynde's hand

again. "We must not fear the worst," she said. "Our sisters are as savvy as you, Rose, else I'd not be here today, and you... you, my dear sister, you would never have found me." She shook her head with a look that betrayed both grief and wonder. "And to think you endured so much. I must thank Giles for taking such great care of my littlest sister, and I will be sure the kitchen prepares him something special."

Now it was Rosalynde's turn to blush, and she did so fiercely, even as she lifted a thumb to her lips in dismay. "Aye well, as to that... there is something else you should know." And then she told Elspeth all about their bonding... about Rhiannon... about the night they spent at Neasham.

"I see," said Elspeth, but if Rosalynde had expected her sister's censure, it wasn't forthcoming. Elspeth gave Rose a sly smile. "I should be the first to say virtue is prized far too highly. You must follow your heart, Rose, and the Goddess will bless you for it. Our sister will doubtless forgive you." And then her smile returned, even brighter. "Come," she demanded again, taking one of Rosalynde's hands and pulling her again down the hall. "I will show you the rest of my home later, but now I really need to show you something..."

27

T he *something* Elspeth needed to show her wasn't a cauldron at all—and now that she stood gazing upon the marvel, she understood why her sister had dragged her away so hastily and insistently...

Two small babes lay swaddled in a crib, both fast asleep. One had the look of their mother, with pale coppery hair. The other had hair so fair that it could have been spun silver. Both their cheeks were round and high with color as they lay sleeping near a brazier. The woman who'd been tending them moved away to give her mistress privacy, and Rosalynde's heart swelled with joy as she gazed down at the sleeping pair. "Yours?" she asked with wonder.

"Born on the Solstice... whilst in Scotia. They came early, though it did not seem so. I was quite ready to be done."

It was clear by the look in her sister's eyes that she was content—more content than Rosalynde had ever imagined.

"We went to celebrate the Yule with my husband's family, and, that night, I went into labor. This was two months ago."

"Twins," Rosalynde said with wonder, as she studied the babes, shocked that both had come from her sister's womb. Instinctively, she put a hand to her own belly... Twins were a Pendragon blessing—or curse, so their mother would have them believe, for she, herself bore two sets of twin girls: Arwyn and Rosalynde, of course, but before them, she had carried another set. Only one of those girls lived. That babe was Rhiannon.

"Such beautiful girls," Rosalynde whispered.

Elspeth burst into laughter. She put a finger to her lips, stifling her mirth. "*Never* say such a thing in their father's presence. He would cut out your tongue!"

Rosalynde tilted her sister a questioning look. "They are not girls?" The blessing was nearly always girls.

Elspeth shook her head, grinning behind her finger. "Boys, to my husband's delight—and, you my dear, should have seen his father when those lads arrived. Sweet Goddess save me! Never in my life did I hear such a whoop and holler in a house."

Rosalynde giggled. "Well, I suppose it would be a matter of pride to father boys—and not one, but two." She reached down to touch the air before the redhead's nose, afraid to disturb either one. They were sleeping so blissfully, without a care in the world.

"Broc and Lachlan," Elspeth provided. "The fair one is named for a beloved uncle—a man called Broc Ceannfhionn. Alas, though I did not meet this man whilst in Chreagach Mhor, I have been promised a visit."

With a look of perfect rapture on her face, she reached down to smooth her hand across the sleeping babe's cheek. "The name, I am told, means Broc the Blonde... and he should be so fortunate if he receives the blessings of his namesake." Elspeth turned to face Rosalynde. "He is lord of Dunloppe."

"I don't know Dunloppe," said Rosalynde, but it didn't matter. Whilst she stood, gazing down at her sweet nephews, she felt in her heart that all things would end as they should end. No matter how much terror lived in this world, the Goddess would not bring such perfect little beings into this realm without hope —*sweet fates*, she was an aunt and Elspeth a mother!

In the midst of so much heartache and peril, there was still so much joy to be found!

Both babes were so astonishingly beautiful, and whilst the red-haired child's face so much resembled his mother's, the other one... the fairest child... seemed to glow. His countenance was precisely how Rosalynde always imagined the radiance of Taliesin to be. The babe's skin was iridescent, his nose perfect, his lips so rosy in color, his brows tipped with a gold so pale... She stared at the boys, comparing them, as it would be natural to do. After all, she herself was a twin, and she knew how different twins could grow to be... and yet, how much alike. At the instant, she missed Arwyn more than words alone could say.

"He looks to be the image of Emrys," Elspeth said.

"Emrys?"

"Our uncle, who died before Rhi was born. I never met him, though Grandmamau described him just so."

"Emrys," Rosalynde said again, whispering the name as she tried harder to remember. But, alas, there was no memory for her to draw upon, because her grandmamau had been long dead by the time Rose and Arwyn were born—murdered by Huntsmen, though she mustn't think of that right now... not now, when the man she loved carried the same serpentine sword as those men who'd arrested Morgan Pendragon and sentenced her to death... not when she had hopes to bear his children, even knowing what he was...

Alas, that was something she had yet to tell Elspeth, and she dreaded the moment, because, so much as she could never keep such a thing from her sister, she also knew how much Elspeth had loved their grandmamau. It was bound to color her feelings about Giles.

Giles!

Peering up at the window to gauge the time, she realized with a start that they had left Giles waiting so long. She should return to him now, introduce him to Elspeth. She wanted desperately for them to know each other, before she dared to tell Elspeth what he was.

Her heart longed for him, even now—even as she wallowed in the joy of her reunion with her sister.

Her sister hadn't any notion of the turmoil that raged in Rosalynde's heart. "It occurred to me, Rose... according to Grandmamau, Emrys was a *dewine*," she said, her voice soft and sweet as she petted her boys in turn. "Evidently, not only did Emrys look like the prophet Taliesin, he was blessed with his *dewine* gifts as well."

There were very few *dewine* males in the world— very, very few. Normally, these gifts were passed to girls, and even then—as was the case with Arwyn, sometimes the *gift* was not strong. However, when a *dewine* male was born, it was prodigious... Suddenly, noting the boy's shimmer, Rosalynde blinked, as she looked up to ask, "Elspeth... do you think..."

Elspeth smiled radiantly, though she still didn't

look at Rose. At the moment, her eyes were for her boys alone. "That he has our gifts?"

Rosalynde nodded, and her sister shrugged, unconcerned one way or another. "Only time will tell," she said, and then reached across the crib to cup Lachlan's sweet cheek, her violet-blue eyes radiant with love. "Every time I think of our mother," she said, with no enmity at all, "I turn my eyes to my babes, and they give me such faith. After all, how could there not be hope for all when I know the miracle of my sweet boys?"

They were, indeed... two sleeping miracles, and Rosalynde might have been content enough to stand and stare at her nephews for hours longer... but she heard a horn blast, and a stab of fear entered her heart.

Elspeth started, her eyes widening, and she said breathlessly, "Malcom!"

28

Not only had the lord of Aldergh *not* returned from his council at Carlisle, Giles was gone now, as well. With the steward's permission, he'd requisitioned two men from Aldergh's garrison, and before leaving, presented the reliquary and *grimoire* to Cora's husband for safekeeping, explaining that the items were priceless and every care should be taken to safeguard them. In turn, Alwin presented the items to Cora, and Cora handed both the book and reliquary to Rosalynde, looking perfectly confused over their value. To her undiscerning eyes, the reliquary would seem to be little more than a brass bauble, and the book must have appeared a dirty volume with the look of a Holy Writ, only with yellowed pages and vellum that was already cracked and blackened with age.

Her heart tripping with the news that Giles had so easily departed—essentially abandoning her at Aldergh—Rosalynde took the book and gave it to her sister.

At least the book was safe, and truly, that's what mattered, she told herself, and yet, her heart felt as though it might be rent in two, and Giles still had the lion's share.

Despondent though she was, she understood Elspeth's intake of breath as her fingers touched the sacred volume. Its hallowed pages must be more than five hundred years old, but the spells and recipes held therein were easily a thousand or more. Not since Elspeth was a small girl had she laid eyes upon their grandmother's *grimoire*, and, in truth, until they'd arrived in London, none of the sisters had ever even looked upon it. Only Elspeth had ever had the chance to hold it and open it, under the supervision of Morgan Pendragon.

"We *must* keep it safe," Rosalynde entreated. "On pain of death. Mother must never see the Book of Secrets again."

"I have precisely the place to keep it," Elspeth reassured, and then led Rosalynde to her salon, to a corner of the chamber, where the floorboards were loose. She lifted a board, and set the book beneath, then replaced the floorboard, and peered up at Rose while still on her knees, her blue eyes full of concern. And it was in that instant Rosalynde weakened.

Tears sprang to her eyes—tears she could no longer deny. "He's gone, Elspeth," she said, her face twisting with grief.

Her sister's brows slanted unhappily as she rose to her feet, embracing Rosalynde, putting her warm, comforting arms about her. "Here, here," she said. "I am here, Rose. Do not fret. I am here." And she let her sister comfort her, sinking like a hopeless child into her consoling arms.

So many weeks she'd traveled to arrive here, so much peril she'd endured—she and Giles both together. But now he was gone. *Gone.* And he had ridden away to see to his own affairs without so much as a bittersweet so long.

CARLISLE CASTLE LAY but an easy half-day's journey
from Aldergh. The jewel of Cumberland was impossible to miss, with its fiery red stone and enormous
girth.

Having gathered his most trusted advisors to dis-
cuss his new stratagem—a possible siege of York—the
king of Scotia was in residence, sequestered behind
closed doors. Giles needed only present his Paladin
sword, with the serpentine emblem, and he was ad-
mitted at once.

Without a word, he took an empty seat among the
men gathered and listened quietly as the Scots king
carried on about the strengths and weaknesses of York
and the benefits of controlling the archdiocese there.
Already, he held Bamburgh, Newcastle and Carlisle,
and Giles suspected that, if he could, he would bring
the entirety of the ancient kingdom of Northumbria
under his dominion. Regrettably, he would soon learn
that the Church would not sanction this plan. There
was already a plan in motion, and it did not include
negotiations with yet another contender, regardless of
David's intentions or associations.

David of Scotia was well respected by the Church,
else he'd never have been brought into the inner sanc-
tum, but that didn't matter. And now that Rosalynde
and her book were both safe, he had a job to see to,
and, knowing what he knew now, there was all the
more at stake—not merely the fate of a northern estate, or even a kingdom.

As God was his witness, he'd never coveted Warkworth for the sake of a title. His father had earned the
lands through sweat and blood. He'd answered every
call to arms by King Henry, and he'd raised his sons to

honor England and its God-appointed sovereign. And even after Stephen usurped the throne, Richard de Vere had been prepared to keep the King's Peace. It wasn't until very recently that he'd turned his eyes toward the Empress, aligning himself with Matilda, and Giles had had a hand in that matter. When the Church asked him to approach his sire in the name of the Empress, he had done so without reservation. He had convinced the elder de Vere to join their cause. This, after all, was why Wilhelm was sent to Arundel, in order to convey their father's answer to Henry's widow, who secretly passed his answer to Matilda. Giles suspected that Lady Arundel's husband discovered the correspondence and immediately dispatched one of Morwen's ravens—those bloody aberrations. It would have flown directly to its master, not to Stephen, and unfortunately for Warkworth, Morwen and Eustace had been only a few leagues from Warkworth when the message arrived. After his resounding defeat at Aldergh, the king's incompetent son had endeavored to assuage his puerile ego by teaching the wayward lord of Warkworth a lesson, putting his "adulterine castle" to the torch, with innocents still asleep in their beds. Ultimately, Giles felt responsible for the entire ordeal, and if it were possible, he would have handed Warkworth to his brother lock, stock and barrel.

Right now, he needed the lord of Aldergh's help, but evidently, this was no longer a matter of one defender of the realm appealing to another. Malcom Scott was no longer Stephen's man... he was David's— quite clearly, because here he sat, divulging York's weaknesses and expounding upon the complications of wresting York from the English. And yet this was far more complicated than even Malcom realized.

Although William FitzHerbert, the king's nephew, had been deposed and the succession to the archbishopric was still in question, the Pope had yet to decide between Henry Murdac and Hilary of Chichester. The king's choice was Hilary, and he had already endeavored to deprive Murdac from taking up residence in the city of York, but he was currently negotiating with the Pope. He would give Murdac the archbishopric if only the Pope would agree to coronate his son. The Pope was not in the frame of mind to do so, and yet, neither would he accept a third candidate for the archbishopric, when he had already decided upon Murdac. At the moment, a siege of York would be met with opposition, not only by Stephen, but by the Church as well.

Considering how best to proceed, he waited patiently for his opportunity to speak, then put forth a request: He needed stone to rebuild. He would pay well, and because Warkworth lay so close to the Scots border, he sought the Scots king's blessings. But, of course, David saw an opportunity and seized it. He offered Giles the chance to retain his title... if only he would give his allegiance to Scotland instead of England. If he should agree to it, he could have all the stone he needed without question, and there would be no risk of losing his lands or, for that matter, his title. David would confer it to him now, on the spot.

A shocked murmur swept through the council. For all that these fools knew, Giles was a younger son of a lowly baron, with no experience and scarcely any influence. It was unthinkable what David had proffered, and yet... Giles could not and would not accept. He shifted in his chair, ill-at-ease, because there was so much he hadn't leave to say, and the council room was filled with too many curious ears. His gaze skittered down the table, from man to man, resting for a moment on the lord of Bamburgh, whose youngest daughter was wed to his father and had died by Eustace's hand. There was no love lost between their houses, despite the familial alliance, because Bamburgh bent the knee to David. But for Giles, this was inconsequential. In essence, he was only reclaiming his father's seat by behest of the Church. And if they had not ordained it... he would still be wielding his sword in whatever capacity they demanded. That he was now a lord of the realm—an earl for the time being—did not come without obligation. There was only so much he could bargain with and keep the spirit of his oath.

He chose his words carefully. "I do not need warriors, Your Grace. I have warriors. I need stone, and whatever men would be required to convey and work the stone. It is my intent to restore Warkworth to a defensible state as swiftly as is humanly possible—most certainly before I am expected to return to London and bend the knee to Stephen."

"Do you plan to forswear your oath to Stephen?" asked David quite shrewdly.

Giles said naught, for there was naught he could say. He picked at a bit of dried foodstuff encrusted upon the table.

"It sounds as though you mean to forswear England, and if so, who else would you bend the knee to, but David?"

Giles flicked a glance at the lord of Bamburgh but didn't answer the man. His gaze returned to David.

More than any man present, Giles knew that David understood the significance of his Papal commission, and yet David mac Maíl Choluim was king because he pressed his advantages when he saw the opportunity.

"Whatever the case, I haven't men to spare," he persisted. "And yet... I would offer... if only you bend the knee to Scotland."

Giles shook his head, his eyes never leaving the king's. "I cannot give what is not mine to bestow."

The tension in the room was marked. In this day and age, few men dared to defy David mac Maíl Choluim. He had risen to such a venerable position. And yet, *one* man did speak up—a very unexpected ally, and only by virtue of the fact that Giles had arrived with two of his men. "I can spare you whatever men you need," said Malcom Scott.

His brows colliding fiercely, David shifted in a chair that was made for lesser men, turning to spear Malcom with a disapproving glare. "*You* have men to spare? And yet, even knowing my plans, you would offer them to Warkworth?"

Giles recognized the hard glimmer in Malcom Scott's eyes. As would be expected, he was a man not easily cowed. He said, "I have given you my oath, Your Grace, and I mean to keep it."

"This time," interjected the earl of Moray.

"Shut your gob, fitz Duncan!"

Uncowed, Malcom met de Moray's gaze and said, "I have given my sword to Scotia, and I will honor my pledge for the rest of my days." He turned to the king. "Your Grace, would you leave Aldergh without protection, or have me arm bricklayers and quarrymen?"

"Nay," said the king, waving a hand for peace.

"And yet *these* are the men I would pledge to my lord of Warkworth, not my warriors."

The king conceded. "Yeah, times are not so dire as to send bricklayers into the field—have it your way."

As much as he would like to cede, Giles was forced

to disagree. "Do not mistake me, Your Grace. Times, indeed, are so dire…"

Very slowly, the king's eyes slid back to Giles, his gaze narrowing, "Speak," he demanded.

Giles shook his head again. "I will not speak aloud what I know, lest you lock me in a tower and call me a madman. And even so, I would advise you to gird your loins."

"Gird his loins?" wailed de Moray, in protest, clearly not comprehending his cautionary words.

"He means prepare for war, eegit," said David.

Giles ignored the man. "And nevertheless, Your Grace, I do not need a grant of men. I need stone… and for this I pledge you my word of honor I'll not join any campaign to wrest the lands you already possess."

The king's eyes glittered fiercely. "What of Warkworth?"

"Again, Warkworth is not mine to barter."

"It *is* yours," argued the lord of Bamburgh.

"In name only," returned Giles. "My true oath and my sword belong to the Church, as your king already knows."

David mac Maíl Choluim's gaze fell to the sword hilt that peeked above the table, a sword that, even now, glowed very faintly with some unnatural light. There were twelve men present at David's table—and how prophetic that the king of Scotia should have his own Judas. Alas, there was only one way to ferret out a traitor, and so he said, "The Church means to see Duke Henry on his grandfather's throne, and I will do my part to bring that to fruition."

Giles's canny dark eyes scanned the entire table, from the lord of Bamburgh to the earl of Moray, looking for any telltale sign of the betrayer. Unfortunately, the man did not make himself known, and yet, if the sword spoke true, at least one of these allies would carry this news to Stephen, and the Church would know his name.

Perhaps not entirely surprised, David put a hand to his chin, rubbing softly. "Duke Henry?" he said.

"Aye, Your Grace. He is favored above his mother, and should his foray into Wiltshire have proven successful, he might already have been granted an army."

"And it was not?"

It was phrased as a question, but they already knew what came of that campaign, and for the most part, it came to naught. Giles lifted a shoulder. "His courage did not go unnoticed."

"He has what it takes. His grandmother would have been proud," the king said, sounding maudlin, and it seemed, for an instant, that he lingered in some faraway place. Finally, he declared, "The stone is yours, so long as you pay its rightful lord. If you have a bargain, who am I to contend?"

And still, there was one more matter to be discussed... this one with the lord of Aldergh. "One more thing..."

The king lifted his grey-peppered brows.

"As part of my bargain with Stephen, I am pledged to wed one of Henry's daughters..." He turned his gaze toward Malcom Scott. "Seren Pendragon."

Malcom's brows collided. "My wife's sister?"

Giles nodded, and once again, David waved a hand in dismissal. "Why should any of that concern this council?"

"Because... I would wed another in her stead... her sister... Rosalynde Pendragon."

The king looked confused. "Are these not both Morwen's daughters?"

"They are, Your Grace."

"I see," the king said, narrowing his eyes. "You risk much if you are already forsworn."

"And nevertheless, I will have no other, and it is my desire to be shed of any need for Stephen's blessings by the time I am expected in London. Therefore, I seek your blessing, for what it's worth."

"Again, I ask; why should I concern myself with your bride?" argued David. "You have declared for England. And I cannot be bothered with Morwen's witchy daughters."

Giles narrowed his gaze. "Because, Your Grace... whether you acknowledge them or nay, they bear a king's blood, and so I ask your blessing, as I do the lord of Aldergh's, because it *is* a matter of state. And... you are—were—their father's dearest friend. You must have known that Elspeth Pendragon was the king's favorite."

"Aye, well, I am also responsible for the death of their grandmother, in case you did not realize, and I have *no* regrets. There are forces at work in this realm that must be condemned."

"And still, you came to aid us," reminded Malcom. "It was not me, but my lady wife who called you."

David of Scotia nodded, and after a moment, he said, "So I did. So I did. Well then, for what it's worth, you have my blessing. For what it's worth..."

Giles turned to Malcom. "So then, I have one more concern...do you, perchance, have a priest in residence at Aldergh?"

Malcom's blue eyes glinted. "As it happens, I do. And, if the lady will have you, you have my blessing as well."

29

F or all its lateness, winter descended upon the north with a vengeance not unlike Morwen Pendragon's. Bitter winds howled through the old castle, leaving everyone it touched shivering. Rosalynde discovered firsthand what her sister meant about the tapestries. Wherever they were hung, those rooms were warmer, quieter, and cozier—much in the same manner of a warming spell, except that these *spells* were woven of wool, linen and gilt-wrapped silk.

As it turned out, it was fortuitous for Rosalynde that her sister's twins were wont to come so early, else she might not have returned in time from Chreagach Mhor. Traveling in this weather would seem impossible, and particularly so with two small babes. As it was, she'd delivered them well and spent a good month with her husband's family before returning to Aldergh.

Alas, so brave a soul as one might be, it wasn't advisable to venture beyond their refuge of stone and tapestry. Rosalynde resolved herself not to see Giles for a while—if ever again. She realized he had far more important matters to attend, the very least of which was a woman he'd already hardened his heart against.

And nevertheless, she had, very knowingly, even despite his warnings, given herself to him. And, in the end, if she ended with a babe in her belly and a sullied reputation, it would be her own fault.

Trying not to think of Giles, she spent her time helping Elspeth with her babies—feeding them, burping them, loving them. And whenever the babes were sleeping, she and Elspeth studied every page of the *grimoire*, poring over the annotations—some of which were written by their mother. But some were not. They had been scribed in a hand neither of them recognized and in a script the sisters couldn't understand—runic symbols that shivered over the vellum when they were touched. But perhaps these were destined to remain as much a mystery as the reliquary she'd taken from Mordecai. After all, Rosalynde showed the strange trinket to Elspeth.

Beautifully etched, it was cylindrical in shape, about a half-inch in diameter and one and one-quarter inches long, with a crystal shoved into one end and a cap so tightly fitted it was impossible to remove. And yet, she had witnessed with her own two eyes as Mordecai's spirit—for lack of a better way to put it—vanished into the object, mayhap into the crystal.

The chain itself was a brass ball chain, solidly formed, and if it had not been, Rosalynde would never have been able to clasp it so doggedly in the glade as Mordecai whipped her about, trying to be shed of her.

One evening, as the babes were upstairs asleep in the care of their nurse, she and her sister sat in the privacy of her lady's solar, trying again to open the reliquary. Nothing—not even *magik*—served to meet their needs.

"It's indestructible!" Elspeth complained, and in

frustration, she put the cylinder to her teeth, biting down in an attempt to squash the metal, but even then, it would not bend.

"Do you think it is ensorcelled?"

"Certainly," Elspeth said. "I cannot think our mother would take any chances with something so...." Elspeth set the reliquary down on the desk she used to scribe her letters. "*Precious*."

By now, Rosalynde had told her all she could remember about their journey and their encounter with the Shadow Beast. Even now, it was impossible to guess what might have waylaid Morwen, but they were in accord that whatever it was, it was the only reason Rosalynde and Giles had found their way to Aldergh in one piece.

As they stood there, Rose fell silent, feeling guilty, for keeping one last secret from Elspeth. "Well," she demurred. "Perhaps it is not the *only* reason." It was past time to tell her sister about Giles. "He's a Huntsman," she blurted.

Elspeth blinked. "Who's a Huntsman?"

"Giles."

"Giles?"

Rosalynde nodded.

Her sister inhaled and did not immediately exhale.

For a long moment, they stared at one another, and Elspeth gleaned the rest by the look in Rosalynde's eyes.

"I do not know if he was there... that night when *she* died..."

"Grandmamau," Elspeth said, and Rosalynde nodded, as tears formed in her sister's eyes.

A thousand lifetimes would pass, and her sister might never forget the day their maternal grandmother was burned at the stake. She suffered guilt over it, because it was Elspeth herself who'd sealed her fate. At five, she'd innocently boasted to a stupid little boy that their grandmamau would put a spell on him if he didn't cease to annoy her. The wretch tattled to his papa, who told the Archbishop of Canterbury. And when they approached Morwen for confirmation, their mother assured them that the sins of Avalon would die with her *dewine* mother. For a price, she'd handed her own mother over to the Church to be burned alive.

"One might think a body dies quickly on the stake," Elspeth said, staring at the reliquary on the desk. "It isn't true. I watched... at first, because they made me... and then, in the end, I did not want her soul to leave this realm alone. I held her gaze until she submitted to the flames, and even as her flesh was consumed... I could still see the life in her eyes..."

She bowed her head and covered her trembling lips with a hand, and Rosalynde stared down at the pate of her sister's bowed head. "I wish I could have known her," she said, tears brimming, but she wasn't only crying for her grandmother. Her heart was in tatters.

And yet, what did she think would happen when she gave herself to Giles? Did she think he would forsake himself and his people? His duties? His brother? His name? His title?

Alas, if he kept her by his side, if he publicly forsook Seren, he stood to lose everything.

Finally, when Elspeth's gaze lifted to Rosalynde's, her eyes were shining with tears. "Do you love this man so much?"

Rosalynde nodded, tears streaming down her cheeks. "I do, and I know his heart, Elspeth. It is true. After all, he could have left me to fend for myself, and yet, even after learning who I was, he set his face against all that he was sworn to do and became my champion... as Malcom did for you."

Elspeth nodded, and Rosalynde continued. "That night I gave him my body, I heard Rhi speak to me. She entreated me to do it—in the name of the Goddess. And..." She cast a glance down at her side, thinking about the wounds she had received by Mordecai's talons. "His kiss healed my wounds when my spell did not... I confess, I took it as a sign." She turned her palm up, showing Elspeth the black lines on her hand... marks left by the reliquary. Though lighter now, they were still there.

Elspeth stared at her open hand, her violet-blue eyes so full of compassion. "I have come to understand that the Goddess works in mysterious ways, Rose. After all, even after David of Scotia's hand in our grandmother's demise, I wrote to him at Carlisle... and he came. There is great *magik* to be found in love and forgiveness."

Her sister's gaze fell again to Rosalynde's hand, and she picked up the reliquary, examining it. "I tell you true, if he had not come... that spell I cast would not have saved us from Morwen's wrath. She left the premise *only* because her poppet was in danger, and without her precious Eustace, she could not see her plan to fruition. To speak more plainly still, if David of Scotia had not arrived with his army... I would not be here today, and neither would my boys..."

She peered up at Rosalynde, with another flood of tears brimming in her eyes. "In the end, you must look to your heart and determine for yourself what the Goddess has entreated... for you... and whatever you choose, my dearest sister, neither I, nor Seren, nor anyone who loves you will ever fault you for your choices. I am your sister forever, and I'll not be your judge nor jury."

Rosalynde attempted a smile, but her lips trembled. Because, in the end, what would any of it matter if Giles did not return? If he did not value her as she did him... if he did not...

A great boom sounded below stairs, like the slamming of a door. Elspeth stiffened as a burst of cold air traveled up the stairs and swept into the solar. She set the reliquary down upon the desk as footsteps raced up the stairwell, echoing throughout the keep. A commotion resounded in the hall and a smile lifted her face. "Malcom," she said, and even as she turned, she found her lord husband standing in the door of her solar. Rosalynde watched with bated breath as the lovers ran to each other, embracing.

"Oh, Malcom!" her sister said. "Malcom! Malcom! Malcom!" She hugged her husband so desperately that Rosalynde feared she might cut off his breath, and nevertheless, her husband smiled lovingly at her, rubbing a hand across the small of her back. And, finally, Elspeth wrenched herself away, complaining, "I did not hear the horn announce your arrival!"

The lord of Aldergh met Rosalynde's gaze over his wife's shoulder and said with a smile, "There was no horn. I came through the postern. Every once in a while, I mean to remind my lazy men that not all guests will announce themselves at the gate." And even as he bent to kiss his wife, another figure appeared over Malcom's shoulder, and Rosalynde's knees buckled as the earl of Aldergh stepped aside, pulling his wife with him to give Giles de Vere room to pass.

Rosalynde's throat constricted and her eyes filled with hot tears, and from that instant, it was as though everyone else faded from the room. Dressed in his Warkworth colors, he strode confidently into the room and with purpose, unsheathing his sword as he fell to one knee before Rosalynde. He peered up at her with a light shining in his eyes, and said, "My lady... I cannot promise you lands or titles, but I can offer you the protection of my sword and the eternal flame of my heart.... will you wed this man who adores you more than life itself?"

Rosalynde gasped, her eyes widening, her hand flying to her breast. "What about Warkworth?"

He smiled at her. "If tomorrow they should strip me of everything—my titles, my lands—it occurred to me that I will still be a very rich man..." He took her by the hand, turned it to face him, then gently kissed it. "Because of you."

More tears welled in Rosalynde's eyes and then tumbled down her cheeks, but these were not tears of sorrow. Her heart was so full of joy she feared it would burst.

*Say, aye, s*he heard her sister *mindspeak. Say, aye.*

"Aye," Rose whispered, and Giles rose to his feet to embrace her, kissing her soundly. "Aye," she said again. "I will wed you."

"The destiny of man is in his own soul."
—*Herodotus*

Not for the first time, Rosalynde peered down in wonder at her unblemished palm... free of scars. Like the ones on her midriff and the ones on her heart, her husband's love had healed her. He was The One the Goddess had ordained for her, and she had no doubt remaining at all. She only wished she could lessen his burdens. Her heart yearned for more time alone with him. Even now he was ensconced with emissaries in the marquee they were using as their living quarters during this time of reconstruction.

Seated high atop a motte, on the banks of the River Coquet, less than a mile from the sea, Warkworth castle was slowly but surely rising from its ashes. Completed only yesterday, two sturdy towers now guarded the entrance to the inner bailey, and the curtain wall had been completed as well, twenty-feet thick and solid as the bond she was forging with her new husband. Tomorrow they would begin construction on the *donjon*. Already, the first stones were laid for its foundation—stone that had been quarried from lands belonging to Elspeth's husband. Wearing the blue gown and the matching cloak Giles had purchased for her at Neasham, she stood atop one of the cornerstones, precisely in the spot where Giles had said their bedroom tower should be erected, with windows facing the sea.

Stretching her hand, she peered over the horizon, and tried to imagine what it would be like to peer out her bedroom window on a moonlit evening whilst her husband called to her from their bed... the brazier warming their room, the stars twinkling like fae dust over a black velvet ocean.

From this vantage, even without a tower, the beach was clearly visible. Offshore, waiting for permission to enter the harbor, a new ship waited to dispatch cargo, sails unfurled and the sea stretching endlessly. Not unlike her husband's kisses, the view never failed to steal her breath. As lovely as she imagined Blackwood must be, as much as she someday hoped to see it, and so much as she appreciated the size and edifice of Aldergh, she could simply not imagine a more beautiful place to be than Warkworth—its lady in truth, even if she could not yet shout it to the heavens.

After all, Giles would keep his new title, and he would keep it, not because Stephen ordained it, but because the Church intended to install a champion here at Warkworth—a voice for change and an agent for Duke Henry, who even now was being groomed to restore his grandfather's dynasty.

Only now, months later, Rosalynde understood so much of what Giles could not tell her, and she knew it despite that he had kept his vow of silence. She understood because she and Will had been there as witnesses... on that day, in the woodlot south of Whittlewood and Salcey.

Little did her mother know, Giles was not some lowly lord with so little power or influence; he was a man who governed from the shadows, and his whispers were more formidable than shouts. That ship out there—one of many that came and went so furtively—was a testament to the power her husband wielded. In less than three months, they'd already accumulated more than two years' worth of rations, and there was a secret hermitage under construction for emissaries of the Church, with a chapel carved directly into the stone.

In an effort to forestall hostilities, it had been Giles's idea to put a worm in Matilda's ear... to give Stephen a conciliatory offer: Keep his throne whilst he lived, but pass it off to Duke Henry, instead of his son. In return, Matilda would appease her barons to keep the King's Peace. The proposal would be presented to her at the next council in Rouen, and even now they were discussing the particulars.

As for news from Westminster... with two months remaining before Giles must formally renounce her sister, the London palace was silent as the sword in her husband's belt.

Life was complicated, she realized. Destiny was so much like the forging of a great sword. You melt the steel, brilliant and mercurial, and once poured, you must allow it to settle according to its will. But the cast, as well as the character of the alloy, would determine how the steel cooled. A hundred times the cast might be filled, and a hundred times the alloy would settle. And then, once removed from the die, knowing hands would hone and polish it, and despite the unalterable

sameness of the die, every single time it would pro-
duce a slightly different sword. Where Rosalynde's
choices might lead, she had no clue. But she now understood as she never had before, that she, too, had a
part to play in the story of England, as her sister Elspeth did... as Rhiannon must.

Little by little, she saw the mystery unfolding...

Even as Warkworth was being restored—stone by
carefully laid stone—so, too, would England's tale be
told. But if Elspeth had never escaped the priory, she
would not have met Malcom, and if Malcom had not
been tested, he would never have abandoned the
Usurper. Now, he bent the knee to the Scots king, and
his defection had begun a chain of events that, even
now, continued to weaken Stephen's—and Morwen's
—hold upon the realm. For now, the Book of Secrets
was safe... and that was all Rosalynde could do.

Her gaze was drawn to the figure ascending the
motte, carefully picking his way over the newly delivered stone. "Have a care, Rose," he called. "I'd not see
you come to harm in your own home."

Her home.

His home.

Despite so many lingering worries, the thought
lifted her mood. Eager to see him after the long
morning—to hold him, kiss him—she moved to the
edge of the stone, and threw her arms out, reveling in
the breeze that gave wings to her cloak. "'Tis
beautiful!"

For the moment, Giles made no move to climb to
her height, seeming content enough to stand in her
shadow.

"*You* are beautiful," he argued, with a familiar
gleam in his eyes. It was a game they so oft played, one
that normally ended in a bed—their bed.

"Nay," she said with a grin. "*You* are beautiful."

As it always did, the saucy argument made her husband laugh. But he sobered at once, staring a long while, before opening his palm and producing a small object—a shining ring. Very deftly, like a trickster, he moved it between his fingers, then held it aloft, so Rosalynde could see it.

When she squinted, he leapt up onto the cornerstone, as agilely as a boy. "Wilhelm recovered it from the fire," he said, turning the ring between his fingers, so that the sun glinted off the metal. He turned it slowly, so Rose could examine the depiction of a lion sejant holding in his dexter-paw an axe, and in the sinister, a tilting-spear. It was a sigil, she realized—a smaller, more delicate version of the lord's ring.

"He gave it to me when we returned from Aldergh. I saved it, intending to present it to you... but after."

He had no need to explain what "after" meant. The two of them had wedded in secret, with only her sister, her lord husband and their priest as witnesses. As of yet, Giles had not revealed their God-spoken vows to anyone, save Will, though it was hardly a secret that the lord of Warkworth had returned, if not with a bride in name, then a bride of his heart. Later, once all was made right with her sister, and Warkworth was ready to withstand a strike, he would rebuke the betrothal to Seren, and they would wed again, only this time with the Church's blessing, here before all their people at Warkworth.

"Did you come to tease me?" She asked.

He shook his head. "Nay, my love. I saw you standing here and realized... tomorrow is never promised."

That was true. For now, there was a fragile peace in the realm, and even Will was thriving in his role as steward, but tomorrow promised more discord. No matter how diminished Morwen might be, her mother would stop at naught to see her prodigy seated upon England's throne.

"After all we have been through, you will not be my Ayleth," he said, and reached out to take Rosalynde by the hand, sliding the ring onto her small finger. Rosalynde's heart tripped, knowing what it meant. There was no one who would see this ring upon her finger who would not understand. "It was once my mother's." He gave her a nod. "Now, it is yours, my lady of Warkworth. If you will have it..."

She held up her hand to look at the ring. "Oh, Giles," she whispered. "'Tis beautiful!"

"*You* are beautiful," he argued, and when Rosalynde laughed, he pulled her into his arms, kissing her soundly.

"Yeah, I will have it," she said with glee. "I will have it, and I will have you. And I will have you until the end of my days."

His dark eyes crinkled at the corners, but then he sobered. "Rose... there's more," he said. "There's another reason I gave it now."

"Oh, no. What more?" A feeling like dread doused Rosalynde's joy as he reached back to pluck something from his belt. It was a parchment... bearing the king's seal... already broken. "It came for me whilst we were in council," he said, avoiding her gaze for the moment. "We spoke at length about the implications. Read the letter," he demanded.

With trembling hands, Rosalynde took the parchment, her heart tripping painfully, as she straightened it, then read as he bade her...

To Giles, son of Richard de Vere, heir apparent to Warkworth

It is with a heavy heart that I compose you such dire news. But I shall come straight to the point with an economy of words. In the matter of your betrothed, Seren Pendragon, you are hereby released from your contract—

Rosalynde's eyes widened. She peered up in fright. "Oh no, Giles!"

Giles held up a hand and shook his head, then pointed a finger to the letter, begging her to continue. With a sinking heart, she returned to reading and the very next words gave voice to her worst fears.

As the lady has been unaccounted for now for nearly three months, I cannot, in good faith, keep you to our bargain...

Fearful tears pricked at Rosalynde's eyes. "Seren is gone," she said, though she didn't wait for Giles to speak. Once again, she lowered her gaze to the parchment...

... and nevertheless, if you would agree to honor your oath to the Crown, I will ask you arrive on the fifth day of June to seal your vows. In good faith, I will keep my promise to see you honored as the first earl of Warkworth.

However, in the event you do not appear as summoned, I would assume you have no desire to keep your northern estates, and I will assign the seat elsewhere. To be sure the delegate will be agreeable, I shall assign the transference to my son and his loyal forces.

He would send Eustace? Again? The very fiend who'd burned Warkworth to the ground once already? With an army no less! If that were not a threat, she didn't know what was. The letter was signed...

Subscribed and sealed this twentieth day of April in the year of our Lord 1149. Stephen, Rex Anglorum by the Grace of God, Protector of the Realm and Defender of the Faith.

"Nay," said Rosalynde, stunned, returning the parchment to Giles. And for the first time in her life, she had the most desperate longing to send a raven to Morwen—what about Arwyn? Were both of her sisters gone? Where were they? Together? Dead—but nay, nay! If any harm would have befallen her twin, Rosalynde would know it. She knew in her heart... she would know it. "Nay," she said again, swallowing, because, in truth, they'd never received *any* word, not even from Morwen, and they still hadn't any clue why her mother hadn't pursued Rose to reclaim the *grimoire*.

"What will you do?"

"The only right thing to do. I will go, of course. Were it not for Seren, I would defy Stephen to send his son, but they are bound to reveal more to my face than they have in that letter. Therefore, I would go, if for naught else, to investigate where Seren may have gone."

Rosalynde nodded. So much for their fragile peace. Her fingers sought the ring he'd placed around her finger, wishing that life could be so easy as a fae's tale. "When do you leave?"

"We still have two months. We should use that time to prepare. In the meantime, I know you crave news of your sisters, and I encourage you to use your gifts as you will."

She peered up at him, surprised. "Even with... your emissaries?"

He shrugged. "If the Church is willing to use *magik* in one form, they must accept it in another." He was speaking of the sword, of course—the one he wore in his scabbard. And now she understood why it glowed that day in the glade. It was forged by *dewine magik*—a very powerful *magik* not unlike the sorcery that forged the sword of Arthur.

"Shall I go with you?"

"Nay, Rose. You are safer here, surrounded by loyal men. If you travel with me to London, I will not be able to keep you safe."

Alas, she knew he spoke true. It was here that they had an army to serve them. In London, they would be at the mercy of the king. "Will you kneel?"

He smiled sadly. "Alas, my love, to keep you safe, I would kneel a hundred times over."

And so here it began... somehow, she must get word to Elspeth, and perhaps together they could find a way to reach Rhiannon. Rhiannon would know what to do. Rhiannon always knew what to do.

"What about Warkworth?" she worried, realizing how much work was left to be done. The perimeter walls were complete, but there was still so much work to be completed.

"I would leave it, along with my armies, in capable hands."

"Wilhelm?"

"Nay," he said, shaking his head. "I will dispatch my brother at once, with two loyal men to search for your sisters."

"Thank you!" Rose said, hardly realizing how

much she'd longed to hear those words until she did. "I love you, Giles. I love you so much. Thank you, thank you!" And yet, as happy as it made her, she feared for the castle in his absence—who could be this commander he trusted so well? "Who?" She demanded. "Who will you leave?"

Very tenderly, he brushed the hair from her face. "Who else but you, my lady of Warkworth? You are a Pendragon who knows better than any what your mother is capable of—I would leave you in command of three hundred men, and a ship at your disposal, should you need it. If by chance worse should come to worst, you will board that ship and sail to France. But I warrant it will not come to that."

"But—"

He held up a finger. "Before you gainsay me, my lovely wife, let me remind you that I saw you battle a Shadow Beast, all the while my brother sat on his bum —I know your warrior's heart." And he would leave her in charge of an army? Just like that? A woman? A witch?

"Giles," she protested, "I know nothing of battles nor armies—nor even how to wield a sword."

"Oh, yeah," he said. "I nearly forgot." And he stepped back to unsheathe the sword in his scabbard, then held it out, presenting it to her lengthwise, suspended atop the tips of his fingers. "It served me well, but 'tis only fitting it should serve a Pendragon since the alloy used to forge it was designed by a *dewine* to serve a Pendragon. And before she could speak another word, he said, "Lessons begin on the morrow."

Rosalynde blinked, reaching out to touch the shining metal—perfectly made, perfectly preserved, even after so many centuries.

The sword was imbued by the Merlin of Britain, she realized, the father of their coven... Taliesin.

Very reverently, she took the sword from her husband's hands, and with some effort, she held it aloft, lifting the blade so it pointed skyward, catching the sun with a hard gleam that no doubt shone for miles. It was only then... as the sword stood erect in her hands... that she noticed something she hadn't seen before—a single word inscribed between the serpents... *Caledfwlch*... translated, it meant cut steel... and in the language of the Holy Church... *Caliburn*... or *Excalibor*. Blinking, with sudden realization, she peered up at her lord husband.

He lifted one golden brow, and then shrugged. "Luck of the draw," he said.

What's next for the daughters of Avalon? Turn the page.

UP NEXT IN THE DAUGHTERS OF AVALON SERIES...

FIRE SONG

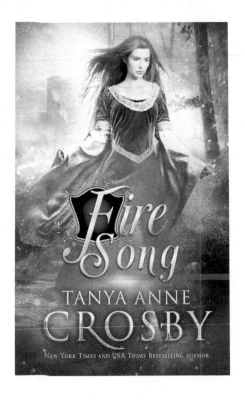

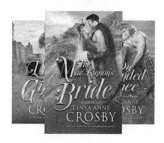

Once Upon a Highland Legend

Highland Fire

Highland Steel

Highland Storm

Maiden of the Mist

ALSO CONNECTED...

Angel of Fire

Once Upon a Kiss

DAUGHTERS OF AVALON

The King's Favorite

The Holly & the Ivy

A Winter's Rose

Fire Song

Rhiannon

ALSO BY TANYA ANNE CROSBY

ABOUT THE AUTHOR

 Tanya Anne Crosby is the New York Times and USA Today bestselling author of thirty novels. She has been featured in magazines, such as People, Romantic Times and Publisher's Weekly, and her books have been translated into eight languages. Her first novel was published in 1992 by Avon Books, where Tanya was hailed as "one of Avon's fastest rising stars." Her fourth book was chosen to launch the company's Avon Romantic Treasure imprint.

Known for stories charged with emotion and humor and filled with flawed characters Tanya is an award-winning author, journalist, and editor, and her novels have garnered reader praise and glowing critical reviews. She and her writer husband split their time between Charleston, SC, where she was raised, and northern Michigan, where the couple make their home.

For more information
Website
Email
Newsletter